"Marielle, you are pushing me to the very edge of my control,"

he admitted, burying his face in the crook of her neck.

"Well then, I'll have to see what I can do to push you past it. I want to see you when you aren't thinking and analyzing everything," she said.

"I'm not sure that's a smart idea," he said.

"I thought we'd decided this wasn't our most intelligent decision," she said, shifting on him to run her finger down the side of his jaw to his mouth. She drew her finger over his lips.

He groaned and shook his head, sucking her finger into his mouth. He needed to take charge but every time he did that he saw the finish line and he wanted...Marielle and this entire night to last as long as it could.

* * *

One Night to Risk It All is a part of the
One Night series.

Dear Readers,

Happy Holidays! I hope you have had a fabulous year. I'm so excited to bring you *One Night to Risk It All* this month. This is the last of the Velasquez brothers, and I'm pretty excited to bring them all to their happily-ever-afters!

Inigo Velasquez lives life at three hundred miles per hour, and he doesn't take his eyes off the track until New Year's Eve when Mari catches his eye. He has no time for a relationship, but some fun fits nicely into his schedule. Mari is just trying to stop acting impulsively, which always leads her to trouble.

Neither realizes that their pasts are linked and the trouble it will cause for them. Inigo is poised to win the Formula One championship this year (only in fiction because no one is coming close to Lewis Hamilton!), and his focus is on driving. When his practice times improve after his one night with Mari, Inigo can't help thinking she might be part of the reason.

I brought back some old favorites from the Moretti Heirs series I wrote a few years ago. Marco Moretti and Keke Hechler are the team owners for Moretti Racing. It's always so much fun to catch up with those characters!

Happy reading,

Katherine Garbera

KATHERINE GARBERA

ONE NIGHT TO RISK IT ALL

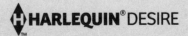

Recycling programs
for this product may
not exist in your area.

ISBN-13: 978-1-335-60407-1

One Night to Risk It All

Printed in U.S.A.

Katherine Garbera is the *USA TODAY* bestselling author of more than ninety-five books. Her writing is known for its emotional punch and sizzling sensuality. She lives in the Midlands of the UK with the love of her life; her son, who recently graduated university; and a spoiled miniature dachshund. You can find her online at www.katherinegarbera.com and on Facebook, Twitter and Instagram.

Visit her Author Profile page at Harlequin.com, or katherinegarbera.com, for more titles.

You can also find Katherine Garbera on Facebook, along with other Harlequin Desire authors, at Facebook.com/harlequindesireauthors.

My parents will celebrate their fifty-second
wedding anniversary on Christmas Eve,
so this book is for them.
They've taught me so much about what love
and marriage and family mean,
and I'm so lucky they are my parents.
Love you both very much!

One

Inigo Velasquez lived life at a fast pace and liked it that way. As the youngest and arguably handsomest of the Velasquez brothers, he enjoyed life to the fullest. No tying the knot and settling down for him. Plus, his career as a Formula One driver kept him on the road and away from his matchmaking mama for most of the year.

He had to give his mom credit, though. It took some real determination to arrange a setup at a party on New Year's Eve, one that wasn't even taking place in their hometown of Cole's Hill, Texas. Back home, Inigo was always on his guard for his mom's maneuvering, but tonight they were all the way across the country at the Hamptons home of his brother

Alec's baby mama, Scarlet O'Malley. Inigo had mistakenly assumed that his mom's network wouldn't be able to produce any potential bridal candidates this far afield.

He had to give her high marks for finding a woman who was hitting all of his hot buttons. She was tall, probably an inch or so shorter than his own five-foot-ten frame. She had long blond hair with some darker streaks that hung down her back. She wore a chemise-type shift dress that was brilliant sapphire blue and complimented her silvery eyes perfectly.

She didn't let her height keep her from wearing heels, and she was by far the most stunning person in the room. She moved through the well-heeled, moneyed crowd with ease, which made him wonder who she was.

"Mom, you've outdone yourself," he said as his mom came over to him with a glass of champagne in each hand. She handed him one, which he took and knew he'd have to nurse all night. He was already training for the upcoming season, and that meant watching his alcohol intake.

"Thanks, sweetie," she said. "It's really only a glass of bubbly."

"I meant the woman," he said.

"What woman?"

"Are you seriously going to pretend that the only single woman in the room isn't here at your behest so that I accidentally meet her?" he asked.

"Inigo, I didn't invite anyone for you to *accidentally* meet. I wanted my boys to settle down in Texas. But Mo is the only one who married a Cole's Hill girl. Diego divides his time between London and Texas, and it looks as if Alec is going to be doing the same, commuting between New York and home. I want my boys close so I can spoil my grandchildren," she said.

Inigo couldn't believe how he was the only Velasquez brother still single. Diego, his eldest brother, had married British legacy jewelry designer Pippa Hamilton-Hoff. Alec had Scarlet, and Alec's twin, Mauricio, was now engaged to his long-time on-again, off-again girlfriend, Hadley.

"So, she's not for me?" he asked.

His mom shook her head and started laughing. "Honey, it's amazing that with your ego and inflated head you can even get the helmet on at the start of a race."

"Ha-ha, Mom. You know it's not that far-fetched that you'd try to set me up," he said.

"I know. Which girl is it?" his mom asked.

He nodded in the blonde's direction.

His mom whistled between her teeth. "She's a looker. How do you know she's single?"

Inigo tried to play it cool, like he hadn't asked around to find out who she was. But his mom, who was watching him, just smiled and shook her head. "You like her?"

"Don't get any ideas," he warned her. "I have a

big year coming up, and I'm focused on being number one."

"I know you are, baby. And your father and I are very supportive of that," his mom said. "But if you like her…maybe you should go and introduce yourself to her."

"I might now that I know you didn't meddle to get her here," Inigo said.

"Might what, son?" his father asked as he came over, putting his hand on his shoulder and squeezing.

"He might go talk to that girl," his mom said. "Here, finish this for Inigo. He's training and shouldn't be drinking."

"Whatever you say, darling," his father said, taking the champagne flute from Inigo's hand. "What a party! Several people have already confused me with Antonio Banderas tonight."

His mom swiped the glass from his father's hand. "Obviously you've had too much to drink if you think that's what they said."

Inigo smiled at his parents joking around with each other. Seeing them together always made him think of relationship goals. But they had gotten together back when life was simpler. Now the world was faster, meaner and more connected. He had to hustle a lot to stay relevant off the track while still winning races on it. There was no time to find someone and get to know them in the real world the way his parents had.

But someday he did want that…when he was like

thirty or, hell, maybe forty, depending on how his career went.

"Which girl are you looking at?" his father asked when his mom spotted one of her favorite Food TV chefs and wandered over. This party had everyone at it, and frankly it was the kind of shindig that he tried to avoid except when his sponsor made him attend.

Sponsors and family. They were the only two things that he ever allowed to pull him away from racing.

"Dad, you can't call women girls anymore," Inigo said. "But she's the blonde in the blue dress over near the French doors."

"You know I meant no disrespect," he said. "Hell, you and your brothers still look like boys to me. Guess it's my age."

"Don't be all aw-shucks with me. If Mom or Bia heard you, you'd be in trouble," Inigo scolded.

"I know. Maybe I'd better go back and find that lady who thought I was Antonio Banderas," his dad said.

"I wouldn't. Unless you want to start the new year with Mom ticked off at you," Inigo said.

"True. How'd you get to be so smart?" his dad asked.

Well, Inigo hadn't been drinking all night, the way his father clearly had, which made everything sharper, but he smiled at his father and winked. "From you."

His father clapped him on the back. "Of course

you did. I like your gir—woman. Have you talked to her?"

"Not yet."

"What are you waiting for, son?" his dad asked. "She's alone. Go."

His father gave him a nudge toward the blonde, and at that moment she glanced over at him to see his father pushing him toward her. Their eyes met, and he knew that he was hooked when she shook her head, smiled at him and crooked her finger.

Marielle Bisset had almost skipped tonight's party. It wasn't her normal scene, but her good friend and fellow social media influencer Scarlet had been insistent that she at least make an appearance and meet representatives from some of the brands that she'd been working with. Scarlet had been her mentor for the last six months. And once she'd realized that the other woman was pregnant, Marielle realized this might be the chance she'd been waiting for.

Scarlet had taken Mari under her wing when Mari had come back from a disastrous year abroad. Scarlet had been more than a mentor to her; she'd been really good at teaching Mari how to accept her flaws and own her past mistakes so she could be a better person.

She'd been slowly growing her YouTube channel and working on increasing her numbers so that she could become a style guru like Scarlet, but it was hard to build that kind of influence. Marielle had been doing it for a little over a year now and felt like she was just starting to find her own place in the noisy world of influencers.

She'd come back to the Hamptons and her parents' home after a disastrous affair with a married man that had left her shattered. She shook her head, wishing it were just as easy to shake off how bad she'd felt when she finally realized he was married. She'd been hiding out in East Hampton for the better part of the last five years in between traveling the world and searching for answers about herself. She'd been making peace with her mistakes, keeping a low profile and building her internet-based influencer business. The scandal and hurt she'd caused had left her broken.

Glancing around the room, she locked eyes with a hot guy who was being shoved in her direction by an older man.

He had dark brown hair, but from this distance she wasn't sure of his eye color. He bore a strong resemblance to the older man, who was laughing. She couldn't help but smile at them. It was clear that they had a strong bond—probably father and son.

Her gaze locked with the man's, and she felt a zing go through her. Dang. It had been a long time since she'd felt anything like that. He looked embarrassed, which was cute, so she crooked her finger at him, and he arched one eyebrow at her as he made his way across the room.

"So someone thinks you should meet me," she said. "But you needed a shove?"

"Uh, no, that's my dad. And he's in full-on party mode," he said, then groaned. "Not that I needed my dad to push me toward you or that I always hang out with my parents."

She just laughed. He seemed so genuine and real that for a moment she wasn't sure he belonged here. "It's okay. Your dad seems like a lot of fun. I haven't seen you at any of the other parties this holiday season, so I'm guessing you're not local."

"No. Texan born and raised. Are you a local?" he asked.

"Sort of. My parents have a house here. I grew up in the city but summered out here," she said. Oh God, she was rambling. But it was totally his fault. Up close she saw that his eyes were a deep, dark chocolate brown and that he had a small scar in his left eyebrow. His jaw was strong and his mouth firm, but he smiled so easily that it distracted her.

"How do you know Scarlet?" he asked.

"She's sort of my mentor. She's been so great about answering all of my questions and helping me to come up with a business plan as an influencer," she said. Scarlet had been the first person to take her seriously when she'd suggested that she wanted to make a career out of social media. Her father had been disappointed that she hadn't landed a husband by now.

But that was her dad. Always making her feel

like a disappointment. Not like this dude's dad, who was watching them and smiling in a sweet way. His dad seemed like a really nice guy. Or maybe a silly drunk, she thought as he turned and moved toward the bar. She realized she'd seen him at the bar a few times tonight.

"Your dad is too funny," she said.

"He's a mess. He's just enjoying the fact that all of his kids are here tonight. Normally at least one of us is away on every holiday, so he's thrilled we all are here."

"That's so cute. Usually it's the mom who's like that," she said.

"Yeah, my mom is a newscaster in Houston, so when we were growing up, she was gone a lot and Dad was the one who did all the school pickups. They are both pretty fabulous," he said. "I'm pretty lucky in that they both made us a priority but weren't too overbearing."

"Must have been nice," she said. As the only daughter in a family of five children, she'd always had a little too much attention from her parents. Her dad had been overprotective when she was younger, but once she was eighteen, he thought that she should find a good man and settle down. He was very old-fashioned about stuff like that.

"What about you? Are you here with anyone?"

"Um, no."

"It might be too forward, but I'm glad you're here and I hope you will be at midnight," he said.

"Nah, I'm happy to be here with you," she said, taking his hand and leading him through the French doors and out on the balcony.

The night air was cold after the warmth of the house, but there were patio heaters stationed every few feet, so it wasn't unbearable. "Why are we out here?"

"I want to kiss you and didn't think I should do that in front of your dad."

He smiled. Damn. He had a really great smile and though she knew she should turn and walk away, there was a big part of her that didn't want to. It was New Year's Eve. Surely she could have one night of fun without it being a big deal, right? One kiss wouldn't hurt.

Right?

She smelled of summer and sunshine as he lowered his head and their lips met. A zing went through him. Was it a warning? But she tasted good, and her lips felt perfect under his. Her kiss wasn't too wet, and she didn't try to shove her tongue down his throat the way so many women he kissed did.

She held on to his biceps, and he couldn't help himself: he flexed his muscles and was pretty sure he felt her smile against his kiss. He had the feeling that he amused her, which was fine with him, because for the first time in a while, he was with a woman who made him feel like he didn't have to try. He could be himself…heck, after his dad shoving him toward her, he'd sort of had no choice but to just be Inigo Velasquez from Cole's Hill, not the up-and-coming F1 star. As a Formula One driver he was always aware of his visibility and he was always focused on winning. For this one night he wanted to focus on her.

He had one hand lightly around her waist, and his fingers flexed as he slowly deepened the kiss. In the distance he heard the sound of the party guests counting down from ten.

He lifted his head. "Got one kiss in this year. I want you to be the first kiss of the new year too."

"That's why I led you out here," she said, tipping her head back and studying him. Her long hair brushed over her shoulder, and he lifted one hand to twirl a tendril around his finger. It was soft and light, as he expected.

When he heard everyone yell, "Happy New Year," he leaned in, brushing his mouth over hers. "Happy New Year."

She kissed him again. None of the tentative teasing stuff he'd been doing, but full-on kissed him. He pulled her closer into his embrace, wrapping his arms around her waist.

Loving the feel of her breasts against his chest and her hips nestled close to his, he pressed his hand against her lower back as she sucked his tongue deeper into her mouth.

He felt his engine roar to life and knew that he was going to get from zero to sixty in a nanosecond with this woman. But they were in public. At a party. A party his parents were attending.

He stepped back, keeping his hold on her waist but breaking the kiss. She looked up at him, a flush on her cheeks and neck, her breath coming in quick bursts. "What's the matter?"

"I think we should get out of here before this kiss gets out of control," he said.

"Is it getting out of control?" she teased, drawing her finger down the column of his throat and running it around the collar of his tuxedo.

A shiver of pure sensual delight went through him.

He was pretty close to saying the hell with it and leading her to the secluded section of the balcony behind the large potted fir tree. But this wasn't some foreign city after a race. This was his sister-in-law's house, where she had family and friends over, and he knew that he had to be discreet.

But then she leaned in, wrapping her free arm around his shoulders, and he forgot about everything but the feel of her in his arms and her mouth under his. Her taste was addictive, and he had the feeling that he might never get his fill of her.

He skimmed his hand down her back. The satin material of her dress was soft but not as velvety as her skin. He cupped her butt and lifted her off her feet more fully into his embrace. She moaned deep in her throat, and his engines roared to life.

Yeah, she had him firing on all cylinders. She

was exactly what he needed tonight. Maybe she was the reason he'd given in to the pressure of his family and come along. He needed this kind of fun. Someone who was here for her own reasons, even if she might be trying to get with him to put another notch in her lipstick case.

Just two people with a strong attraction who wanted each other.

It had been a long time since he'd done this. A little over a year. He liked sex, but women were a distraction and he had been focused on winning. But this was one night. A New Year's gift from the universe.

"Inigo? You out here? Mom needs her New Year's kiss," his sister called from the patio door.

He broke the kiss and stepped away toward his sister, determined to hustle her back inside.

"I'll be right in, Bia. Tell Mom to kiss Dad again. He's definitely in the mood for it," he said.

"He's the one who sent me to find you. Mom won't leave until she's kissed all of her kids."

He heard the woman behind him chuckle and turned back toward her. She wiped his lips with her finger, and he guessed he'd been wearing her lipstick.

"Go on. I'll meet you inside."

He nodded and walked away, still in a sensual haze. The last thing he wanted to do was hang out with his parents, but he knew they were sticklers for holiday rituals.

Bianca linked her arm through his, leaning her

head on his shoulder. "Sorry I had to pull you away from your lady. I think Dad sent me because he knew the boys would tease you endlessly."

"Probably. Thanks for that," he said.

"So who is she?"

He shook his head. "Uh, I didn't ask her name."

"Oh, just went straight for the kiss," Bianca teased.

"Something like that," he said as they reached his parents. He hugged them both and wished them happy new year.

"Happy New Year, Inigo," his father said as he hugged him. "Looks like my instincts were right about you and the lady."

"Dad," he warned his father. His father was usually more subtle than his mom but they both wanted him to find someone and "settle down."

"Just happy to see you smiling off the track," his father said.

"Me too," he admitted.

Then he bade his family good-night and went to find the blonde temptress he'd kissed earlier.

"I don't want to push my luck, but do you want to come back to my room?"

"Yes," she said.

Two

The suite he'd been given at the O'Malley compound, Maison de Houblon, was in a large guesthouse off the pool. It had a great room with a kitchen and living room area and then a large bedroom that had French doors that overlooked the ocean. But tonight, he was more concerned with the view in his arms.

"I don't even know your name," he said.

"Marielle. You?" she asked. There was a lilt to her words, a patrician New England accent that he hadn't really noticed before this moment.

"Inigo," he said.

She leaned back and looked up at him. He wondered what she saw.

"Inigo." She said his name slowly, and he liked the sound of it on her lips.

"Yes, ma'am."

"'Ma'am'? There's the Texas," she said with a wink.

"I'll be honest, you're not going to forget I'm Texan," he admitted. No matter how much he traveled around the world or hung out with the Italian owners of Moretti Motors, he was still a Texas man at heart. He wore designer suits and handmade loafers at all the press events and prerace functions he went to, but in his downtime, when he was at home, he preferred jeans and boots.

"Good. I wouldn't want you to be anything other than what you are," she said, running her hand down his chest, her finger brushing over the studs that kept his tuxedo shirt closed. He felt the warmth of her fingers through the layers of fabric.

"I don't have that ability. In fact, my boss is always telling me to wait five seconds before I respond."

"Why?"

"He keeps hoping that common sense will kick in," Inigo admitted.

"Does it ever?" she asked, running her finger over his bottom lip.

Her touch sent a tingle straight down his spine, making him harden. He pulled her closer, skimming his hands over her hips and holding her loosely. "Nope."

She threw her head back and laughed, and everything masculine in him sprang to attention, demanding he make this woman his. He caught the sound of her laughter with his mouth, kissing her, and feeling alive for the first time in a long time.

He tucked that fact away for later but knew that he was holding someone special. Someone who was making him realize that there was life beyond the track.

He felt her hands between them, her fingers moving methodically. He heard the sound of the shirt studs as they dropped to the floor with a soft pinging noise. He lifted her off her feet and turned, moving backward until he felt the bed behind him, and then he sat down. She stood between his spread thighs, her hands on his shoulders.

"Moving a little fast, aren't you?" she asked in a teasing tone.

"I'm sort of known for my speed," he said, then realized how that sounded. "Not that anyone ever complained."

She just threw her head back and laughed and said, "Did you stick around long enough to find out if they did, speedy?"

"Yes. I'm not a one-and-done kind of guy," he said. It had been a really long time since he'd laughed this much with someone. Spontaneously he put his arms around her body and drew her close, the fabric of her satiny dress scrunching up under his arms. He hugged her to him. Just for a moment he wanted to savor this feeling of lightness. Like there was nothing but fun when it came to this woman.

"What's this?"

"It's just been a while since I've laughed this much," he said. "Thanks."

"You're very welcome," she said, pushing her fingers through his hair and rubbing his scalp as he tipped his head back and looked up at her. "You're different."

"So I've been told," he murmured as her lips came down on his. Their tongues met and rubbed against each other.

She tasted so damned good. He had noted it the first time they kissed, and it was difficult for him to forget. She made him hungrier for more. If hooking up with her made him feel this good, he might have to break his rule about celibacy during the racing season and keep seeing her.

She framed his face with her hands, tipping his head back. The bed dipped as she put one knee on it next to his hips and half straddled him. He fell back on the bed, using his arms around her waist to bring her with him. He liked the way she felt pressed against him from shoulders to waist.

He ran his hands up and down her back, cupping her butt as she deepened the kiss. Though he'd joked about being known for his speed, he'd never been one to rush sex. And it seemed neither was she. She took her time exploring his mouth and moving against him in small subtle movements that made him wish they were naked. But he didn't want to stop kissing her to remove their clothes.

She circled her finger around the back of his ear, rubbing against the side of his neck, which made him so hot and hard that he thought he would explode.

He put his hands on her thighs. Her legs were firm and the skin soft. She wasn't wearing hose, so he was touching her bare skin as he spread his fingers wide and squeezed gently.

She shifted her legs against his as he traced one finger up the back of her thigh. She mumbled something against his lips, but he didn't register the words, just the husky tone of her voice and the way she continued to move against him. Her mouth followed the path of her finger down his neck. His shirt fell open as she moved down his body.

Pushing the hem of her dress up to her waist, he noticed she had on the tiniest black thong. She shifted, kicking off her heels and sitting back as she looked down at his body. He had an intense workout routine to keep in shape. Other athletes didn't always realize the discipline it took to be a driver.

Marielle seemed to like his muscled chest. She pushed the shirt off his shoulders, and he sat up, shrugging out of first one sleeve and then the other.

He had a tattoo on the inside of his left arm that read, If Everything Seems Under Control, You're Not Going Fast Enough. She traced the tattoo and arched one eyebrow as she looked back at him.

"Does everything seem under control?" she asked.

"No, it doesn't," he said, wrapping one hand in her long blond hair and bringing his mouth back down on hers.

He didn't want to talk or think about racing right now. He had been steadily getting better on the track, and a big part of him believed that was because he'd quit hooking up with women, but tonight he didn't want to think about that. It had been too long, she felt too good and it was a new year.

She put one hand between them on his chest. Her fingers spread wide, and her nails scored his skin lightly. He shuddered and felt himself harden further. She eased her hips forward, her center rubbing against the ridge of his erection.

He groaned as his hips jutted up against her. *Oh, damn.* This was going to be harder than he thought. It had been too long since he'd held a woman in his arms, and his body seemed to be on autopilot. Like when he was on the final lap and saw the finish line, he was ready to go. He reached between their bodies, intent on freeing himself, finding a condom and driving himself home inside her.

But the back of his fingers brushed against her underwear, and he felt her heat. She made a little sound at the touch against her intimate flesh, and he turned his hand, cupping her and rubbing just the tip of his forefinger between her legs. She spread her thighs farther apart, and he leaned back to give himself more room as he ran his finger around the edge of her thong panties and then dipped it inside, finally pushing his entire hand into the front of her underwear and caressing her. He parted her, tapping her clit lightly. She moaned, and her fingernails dug into his chest a little deeper. He tangled his other hand in her hair and brought his mouth down on hers.

He kissed her as he continued to tap against her, her hips moving subtly. Then she tore her mouth from his and reached for the hem of her dress, drawing it up and over her head, throwing it behind them.

He saw her breasts, small but perfectly naked, and her tiny nipped-in waist. She reached between their bodies and undid his belt and then slowly lowered his zipper.

"I want you naked," she said.

"Me too. Are you on the pill?"

"Of course I am. I don't like taking chances."

"Me either," he said.

She shifted off his lap, and he pushed his pants and underwear down his legs. By the time he was naked, so was she. She turned back to him, standing there in front of him completely bare, and he took a moment to appreciate how lovely she was. She wasn't built like a supermodel but was more of a real woman. Her legs weren't especially long but seemed just right to him. She had a birthmark on her left side that was shaped like a paint splotch; he couldn't help himself and caressed it, tracing the shape. She had a belly button ring, which he fondled as he used his other hand to draw her back into his arms.

She fell against him, and he rolled over so she

was under him. She put her hands on his waist and then squeezed as she ran her hands down his sides. He honestly wasn't sure how much more touching he could handle before he came on her belly, which wasn't how he wanted this to end, so he took her hands in his and stretched them up above her on the bed.

He watched her carefully to see if this bothered her, but she just winked at him. "Maybe I'll let you tie me up later."

His hips jerked forward at the thought and he could only nod; words were beyond him at this moment. He held her wrists with one hand and drew his index finger down her body, starting at her forehead. She had a pert nose that he couldn't help dropping a kiss on as he drew his touch down farther, over her lips and her neck and then around the full globes of each breast. He lowered his mouth to one of her nipples while he teased the other one with his fingers.

Then he moved lower, tasting her belly button ring with his tongue, and felt her undulate against him as he moved still lower. He fanned his fingers out and cupped her, running his finger around the opening of her body and then bringing it up to tap against her clit again. She shifted against him, her legs going wider as he brought his mouth lower, wanting—needing—to taste her. He had to let go of her hands, but he felt enough in control that he thought that would be okay.

He was wrong.

She tasted better than anything he'd ever tasted

before. He couldn't get enough. His tongue flicked over her and then his entire mouth ate at her most intimate flesh until she shoved her hands in his hair and held his head to her body as her hips thrust upward against him.

She rocked against him again and again and then called out his name as her orgasm rolled through her.

He lifted his head and looked up her body. Her head was thrown back and her chest was heaving, her nipples tight little buds. Her hips were still rocking slightly, and he knew he'd never forget how she looked right now. He moved up her body, letting his chest brush over her mound and then her stomach and her breasts. He braced his weight with his hands on either side of her shoulders. She opened her eyes, looking up at him with that silvery gaze of hers, but up close her eyes were silvery gray.

"Well, hello there," she said.

"Hi."

She twined her arms around his shoulders and leaned up to whisper directly into his ear. "Are you going to take me now?"

His hips moved against her, the tip of his erection finding her opening. He met her eyes and leaned down to kiss her, letting her taste herself on his lips.

"Yes," he said against her mouth as he drew back his hips and drove himself deep inside her.

She was tight when he entered her, and he waited to let her adjust to his size. She wrapped her legs around his waist and lifted her upper body so that her hard nipples brushed against his chest each time he drove into her. He wanted her passion to build to climax again, but now that he was inside her, it was the same as being strapped into the cockpit of his race car—there was no stopping him. The light had flashed green for go, and he had one objective in mind.

He rode her hard, driving into her again and again, and as he felt the sensation running down his back that meant he was closer and closer to his orgasm, he reached between their bodies, flicking at her clit to help her along. She arched under him, her nails digging into his shoulders.

"Inigo," she cried.

The sound of his name on her lips triggered his orgasm and he started to come, thrusting into her until he was empty and drained. She arched against him repeatedly, and when they were both still, he rolled to his side, lying on his back next to her.

The air in the room was cool compared to the heat of her body next to his. He already wanted to be back inside her. He turned his head on the bed and found she was looking at him.

"Was that slow enough for you?" he asked teasingly.

"Yes, speedy. You were just right," she said, rolling close to kiss him. "Want to join me in the shower?"

She trotted toward the bathroom, and he just lay there staring at the ceiling. His mother always said that fate brought people into his path when they were meant to be there. And he was struggling right now not to make this more than a New Year's Eve hookup.

Honestly, that was all he had time for, but something about Marielle made him feel lighter, made him feel...stronger. Like he could conquer anything.

It could be because it had been more than a year since he'd gotten laid, but he wasn't convinced.

"Are you coming?" she asked, leaning around the door frame from the bathroom.

"Yes, ma'am," he said, jumping off the bed and heading toward her.

It seemed like it might be her and not just sex. But then, one night wasn't going to change his life. His mom might be a big believer in fate, but he'd never seen its proof in his life.

He showered with Marielle, taking his time to wash her, making sure he explored all the places on her body that he might have missed when he'd made love to her earlier. They did it again in the shower and then dried off and curled up in the big king-size bed in the guesthouse. He held her in his arms as she slept and watched her. Tomorrow everything would be different. The holidays weren't officially over until January 2, but he had a session at the simulation track and if this was going to be the year he unseated the current champion, then this night was all he'd have with her.

He watched the clock and held her, pretending for a moment that things were different, but as much as he enjoyed having her in his arms, he knew that he wanted something more from life. He wanted the title of champion, and these emotions she stirred in him would distract him from his goal. Something he couldn't allow.

Besides, if they were really fated to be together, then she'd come back into his life at another time.

He drifted off to sleep just before dawn and only woke when his alarm went off at ten in the morning. Marielle rolled over and looked up at him from under tousled hair. "Why is your alarm going off?"

"I have a family breakfast. Do you want to come with me and meet the gang?" he asked. "Scarlet will be there."

"Yes, I think I would. I better dash out to my car and grab my overnight bag so I have something to wear other than last night's dress," she said.

"Why do you have an overnight bag in your car?" he asked.

"Just in case. I liked to be prepared. If I get too tipsy to drive, I can always stay at Scarlet's," she said as she got out of bed and stretched before pulling on her dress.

"I like that dress," he said.

"I do too, but it's really better for nighttime," she said.

"Agreed. Which car is yours? I'll get your bag," he said. She told him, and he went out to retrieve it.

They got dressed together, which was fun. He wanted her again, but he didn't want to give in to the craving, so he forced himself to make do with a kiss and held her hand as they walked to the main house. But as they entered the house, they didn't exactly receive the warmest of greetings.

"Oh my God. Who invited her?" Bianca said, standing up from her seat as they entered the enormous living area. There was anger in her voice. Inigo wasn't sure who Bianca was referring to at first but noticed she was staring at Marielle.

"What's going on?" he asked his sister.

"I should be asking you that. What are you doing with Jose's mistress?"

Three

Bianca… Jose's ex-wife was here? She hadn't seen the woman in more than five years, and she'd worked hard to put that horrible day out of her mind. The moment she'd discovered her lover Jose was married had been one of the worst in her life. Seeing Bianca now, all the guilt and shame came rushing back. There was something akin to hatred in the pregnant woman's eyes, and the look on Inigo's face made it clear he wasn't too pleased to find out she had this connection to his family.

To be fair, she'd had no idea who Inigo was when she'd slept with him, but now seeing him next to Bianca, she put the pieces together. They were obviously related. And she now vaguely remembered that Jose had mentioned he had a protégé he thought would do great things in Formula One. Was it Inigo?

"I guess I should be going," she said.

"Yeah, I think that's a good idea," Bianca said. "Who even invited you?"

"I'm Scarlet's friend," Marielle said.

She knew that the woman had cause to be upset with her, but she wasn't the only one to blame. Jose had told Marielle he was divorced, and she had been stupid enough to believe him. She soon realized it wasn't his only lie when she'd caught him in bed with another woman—a woman he'd been seeing for years. She'd felt like a fool, falling in love with another woman's husband. Seeing Bianca brought back all of those feelings of self-loathing that she'd hoped she'd moved beyond.

"Scarlet's my sister-in-law," Bianca replied.

Of course she was. "Honestly, I had no idea that you would be here. That part of my life was over ages ago, and I'm not proud of my role in what was going on in your marriage."

More people were entering the room, including Inigo's parents, and then Scarlet and her assistant, Billi Sampson, came in. Marielle looked at her friend, who was visibly pregnant and still looked very sleepy.

"Scarlet, thank you for inviting me last night. I'm afraid I have to run this morning, but I'll be in touch later," Marielle said, walking out of the room.

Inigo didn't try to follow her, which was probably

for the best. He had been fun last night, just what she needed to distract her from her own problems. But obviously neither of them had intended for it to be the beginning of a relationship.

Yeah, right.

But she knew that it was over. There was no way she could have any kind of relationship—not that she was looking for one—with the brother of the woman whose husband she'd slept with.

Ugh.

Her mom was always going on about reaping what she sowed, and damn, this was a pretty rotten crop to reap. But this trouble was of her own making. When she thought back to the woman she'd been when she was twenty-one, she cringed. She'd been so shallow. So into her own pleasure and her own life that she had been unable to see past Jose's lies to the family that she was hurting. It wasn't that she was so much wiser at twenty-six, but damn, she was a little smarter when it came to men. Or at least she'd thought she was.

No more hookups with men whose last names I don't know, she thought. *Yeah, let's make that rule one for the new year.*

The engine of her Corvette roared to life. She put the car in Reverse and spun out on the gravel drive as she tried to get away from the house and all the people inside it. But there wasn't a car that had rolled off the assembly line that would go fast enough to take her away from herself.

She had that way of doing this more often than she wanted to. She knew it wasn't her fault—how in the world had she ended up at a party with Jose's ex-wife? That was never supposed to happen. She'd followed the teachings of a well-being guru, who had advised her to write a letter apologizing. The guru had said that would bring forgiveness from the universe.

Marielle thought she needed a refund, because all she could see as she raced down the road was the look on Bianca's face as she'd recognized her, and it certainly hadn't resembled forgiveness.

She pulled into the drive that led to her family's mansion and slowed the car, fumbling on the visor for the garage door opener. She parked the 'Vette next to her father's classic Porsche and sat there for a minute, realizing that she was on the edge of tears.

She took a deep breath, fumbling in her purse for her phone and that meditation app that her brother had gifted her for Christmas. She opened it and closed her eyes, listening to the soothing voice and pretending the heat on her cheeks was the sunshine the app's moderator was talking about and not tears.

But in her heart the truth was strong, and she knew that she hadn't forgiven herself for those long-ago mistakes. Thank God she hadn't run into Jose's son. The little boy his wife had been pregnant with while he'd been telling Marielle that she was his soul mate. If she'd been older...

Or not as dumb, she thought.

This wasn't working. She dashed her hand over

her cheeks and turned off the car, getting out and standing there for a minute. She smelled cigarette smoke and looked up to see her eldest brother, Darian, standing there watching her. "I wasn't spying, just giving you space."

"Thanks," she said, walking over to him and taking the cigarette from his hand, dropping it on the ground and putting it out with the toe of her shoe.

"You're supposed to be quitting."

"I know. I didn't take a drag, I was just holding it," he said. "What's up with you?"

"Ran into one of my past mistakes this morning. It's hitting me harder than I expected," she said.

"Why? You know you're not that woman anymore," he said.

Why?

She shrugged, but Inigo's face danced through her mind. She'd liked him. He'd been fun, and he'd made her feel like she was enough.

"What were you doing with her?" Bianca asked as she and Inigo watched Marielle drive away.

"She's the girl…the one I told you about last night," he said, trying to put together the two images he had in his head. Jose's mistress had always seemed someone cold and calculating. While he had never seen his brother-in-law with the woman, he had assumed that she'd manipulated Jose into the affair. Jose had been his idol. Inigo had wanted to be Jose when he grew up. But this…

Marielle hadn't seemed like the type of woman… who would what? he asked himself. Cheat? Have sex with a man? She'd been fun, and he hadn't thought of anything but the heat between the two of them. He had put it down to a year's worth of celibacy, but honestly she was hot and sexy and he had wanted her again this morning. Maybe that was what had caused Jose to cheat.

"Her? Couldn't you have picked anyone else?" Bianca asked.

Inigo's heart was breaking at the pain and humiliation he heard in his sister's voice.

"I had no idea who she was to you, Bia."

"Fair enough. But I never want to see her again," Bianca said. Just then Derek Caruthers entered the room, rushing to his wife's side.

"Bianca, are you okay? I'm sorry I wasn't here with you."

"It's fine. I'm glad we're leaving this morning. I'm ready to get back home," she said. "I never thought I'd see her again."

"I'm sorry," Scarlet said. "I had no idea you two knew each other or the circumstances. Did you know?"

She pivoted on her husband, Alec, who just wrapped his arm around her and hugged her close. "Of course I knew he'd had an affair with Marielle. I didn't know you knew her."

Inigo just walked out of the room. He was angry. All of the emotions that he'd felt when Jose had died, and he'd learned the truth, came back. He knew that wasn't a healthy space for him to be in and ignored his father's calls and his brothers as he first walked and then ran back to the guesthouse where he was staying. He changed into his running gear and left the house through the glass doors that led to the beach. He was vaguely aware that it was cold, and a light rainy snow was falling, but he didn't feel any of it.

He only heard the pounding of his feet on the pavement of the path that was empty on this wintry January morning. He concentrated on each step, trying not to allow any thoughts in his head, but it was hard to keep them out.

He had always had a gift for attracting relationships that were toxic, but this had to totally take the cake. He'd found the one woman in the world he really couldn't be with. It would destroy his family if he was with her.

And yeah, it had been a fun hookup, but there was another part of him that wondered if this was his way of making sure that nothing distracted him from racing. From winning. He'd always been the kind of athlete that pushed everything aside to win. And he was close to being the champion, which had been his one goal since he'd started in the Formula One junior program at fourteen.

He also felt the pain of realizing that his idol had feet of clay. That he was human and real and that he hadn't been perfect. The cold air felt like a blade in his lungs as he continued to run, and he veered off the path and into the small town, where everything was closed. No one was out this early on New Year's Day.

Just him.

Just the man who had too much on his mind and no easy way to sort it out. Should he just let Marielle go? Should he try to get vengeance for Bianca? He couldn't help it, but that thought had entered his mind. Maybe it was that he felt she'd fooled him too. She had to know who he was. But how could she have? He'd been on a different circuit that year when Bianca had been pregnant and Jose had cheated.

Many times Inigo had wondered if he'd still been shadowing Jose, would his brother-in-law have thought twice about cheating?

At the end of the day, was he to blame? He'd pursued winning at any cost, and had turning his back on Bianca and Jose that year been part of the other man's downfall?

He had no way of knowing. Jose was dead, and Bianca had never wanted to talk about it.

He stopped running, leaning forward to put his hands on his knees, his breath still sawing in and out of his lungs. His exhalations were loud in his head but didn't drown out his thoughts. He could fix this. Make up for anything he might or might not have done back in the day.

He could have Marielle and publicly dump her. Would that even bother her? She'd been a married man's mistress.

But even as the thought formed, he knew that it

didn't matter. She needed to know that the Velasquez family weren't to be toyed with. The rational part of his mind warned that there was more to the story than he knew. That the "facts" he had came from the dirt that Alec had dug up on her on the internet. Most of the mistresses had been named but Marielle hadn't been on the list.

But he could only listen to his gut and his heart. His heart remembered the paleness of his sister's face as she'd seen him standing next to Marielle. His gut remembered the strident tone that Marielle had used before walking out. His body remembered her twisting under him the night before.

He could have it all. The woman he lusted after and revenge for his family.

Hiding at her parents' house wasn't ideal. The maids were in and out of her room, her mom sent a tray with lunch, and then her dad knocked on her door. And finally, Marielle faked needing to visit a friend having an emergency and left. Her brother was in the garage again when she came downstairs, and she got it. She wished her problems were as easy for the world to see as Darian standing there with an unlit cigarette. But hers were different.

She was the one with a weakness for men and making dumb choices…could that be called addiction too?

She left in a cloud of muddy snow as she sped away from her problems. There was a wistful sort of regret that engulfed her as she got on the Long Island Expressway and headed back toward Manhattan.

Dang.

This must be how Inigo felt when he was racing. There was a certain freedom from everything but the road and concentrating on the path ahead of her. Maybe she should take up driving professionally.

As soon as the thought popped into her head, she hit an icy patch and her car hydroplaned for a minute, fishtailing wildly on the road. She took her foot off the gas as she saw her life flash before her eyes.

Damn.

She slowed the car and pulled onto the shoulder. Her hands were shaking, and her heart was racing. She didn't want to die. She sat there. The silence in the car made her ears ring, and finally she turned on the radio. "About Last Night" was playing, so she flipped the station and heard Debussy's "La mer." Yeah, classical was good. Just what she needed right now.

She dug into her purse and found her phone. Scarlet had texted her.

Are you okay? I wish you hadn't left like that.

What could she say?

I'm not great. I'm sorry. I could tell I was freaking her out, and you know I'm not good in those situations. I hope I didn't make things awkward for you.

Scarlet and Siobhan had been the first women friends she'd genuinely had in years, and she hadn't wanted to screw it up. But maybe she had. Maybe she should stop trying and just enjoy the train wreck that was usually her life.

You didn't. Well, it was awkward, but I feel like both of you were freaked. If you want to talk, I'm going to be in the city until Friday. Let's have coffee...by that I mean you drink the coffee and I smell it and pretend that I'm having some.

Marielle felt a wave of relief go through her.

Thank you. I'd love that. I'm heading back to New York now. My parents' house was stifling. I'm sorry again for this morning.

I know the feeling. No problem. Can't wait to catch up.

She tossed the phone back into her bag before she asked for Inigo's number. A part of her felt like she should say something to resolve the situation with him, but another part—the smarter part—knew there would be no resolution. She could keep him in her memories as a fun night. And that was all.

Her phone rang, and she glanced at the caller ID. It was her friend Siobahn Murphy, who was the lead singer of Venus Rising. The two liked to party together, and she was always down for a good time. Just what Marielle needed at this moment.

"Hey, girl, happy New Year," she said as she answered the speakerphone and got back on the road.

No more driving fast to outrun her problems. She sat in the slow lane going a respectable speed.

"Hiya. Scar texted me," Siobahn said. "What the hell happened?"

"I'm not sure. I mean, I met this cute guy and he was funny and flirty. Even his dad was funny, encouraging him to talk to me. We kissed at midnight…it was hot," Marielle said. More than hot. It had made her see him as more than a hookup. She had to be honest with herself. She hated the way things had ended with Inigo. But she doubted there was any way back from the current situation.

"Yeah, and then?"

"Then one thing led to another, and I spent the night with him," she said.

Siobahn wasn't fishing for lurid sex details. But there was no way to explain the thing without mentioning that.

"Then this morning he invited me to breakfast with his family, and I knew Scar would be there, so I was, like, sure," Marielle said. Then she walked in and saw Jose's wife staring at her like she was the most loathsome woman on the face of the planet… Maybe she'd skip mentioning that bit to Siobahn. "And…"

"I know. You don't have to say it. I'm in Manhattan. Come to my place. We can eat ice cream or drink wine or do whatever you need. Don't go to your place alone," Siobahn said. "You need someone to remind you that you aren't that woman anymore."

"Thanks," she said. She had changed a lot from who she'd been at twenty-one, and it had been a long hard road with lots of pitfalls. But she had changed. She hadn't made peace with all of her past, but one thing she had made were good friends like Siobahn. She'd been the one who'd introduced her to Scarlet and had started her on this path.

"I'll text you when I'm close."

"I'll be here. I'm eating leftover ham, which isn't healthy, but I'm a bit hungover," Siobahn said.

Marielle had to laugh. She didn't drink like that anymore but remembered those days. She hung up with her friend, realizing that Bianca might never forgive her, but Marielle had to find a way to forgive herself. She couldn't keep beating herself up for old sins.

Not saying it would be easy, but she was going to definitely make that one of her resolutions.

Four

The weather this first week of January reflected Marielle's mood as she left her building on the Upper West Side. It was bitterly cold with a messy sleet and rain falling. The doorman held an umbrella over her head as she dashed to her waiting car. Her driver held the door open as she slid onto the leather seat and the welcome heat. She thanked them.

Scarlet had been true to her word and helped her out despite the fact that it must have caused friction with her new in-laws. But then again Scar knew what it was like to be the center of negative attention. They'd grown up in similar worlds, Marielle thought.

But even career pluses couldn't take away the ache inside when she thought of that encounter with Bianca. It wasn't that she'd really considered Inigo to be a guy she wanted in her life. For all she knew, they might not even be compatible. He might be one of those guys who drank beer out of a bottle and didn't use a coaster…or something like that. But the fact that she didn't get to let it fall apart the way her relationships always did…that bugged her. That had to be what was bothering her.

But she couldn't miss a guy whom she'd slept with one night and that was it.

She wouldn't let herself.

She wasn't that girl.

She had never needed a man after Jose. He'd changed that dream of hers. The one where she met a guy and he swept her off her feet and they lived some sort of fantasy life providing her a Disney Channel–perfect family, not the messed-up one that was hers. But she'd learned that she was better on her own.

Men were fun.

Inigo had been fun.

Until…

But that was in the past and she was moving on. She had an interview with a lifestyle brand that wanted to work with her. She had a manager who had worked hard to get the appointment for her, and she was glad for it. She'd even gone all in and dressed like Blair from *Gossip Girl*. She wanted to look the part of what they wanted. On every influencer account she'd checked out, the look was a mix between Jackie O and *The Official Preppy Handbook*.

The heels she wore were designer, but her manager said if she wanted the work, she needed to make a decision to either flaunt her family name or hide it. She couldn't use it when she wanted to and then drop it when she didn't.

So she'd decided to use her middle name instead of her last name and pretend she wasn't part of one of America's richest families. She didn't want to rely on the name. She'd seen what it had done to her brother Darian. Holding an unlit cigarette in the garage and looking like a trapped animal. But her brother believed in the family mission statement and would do whatever Carlton instructed.

Marielle and Carlton had never gotten along. As her father's trusted right-hand man, he'd been the one to step in and divert the media attention from her after the affair with Jose had been made public. He'd quieted things down and done his magic to keep her out of the spotlight. But she still didn't like him. He always wanted Marielle and her brothers to present this perfect Kennedy-esque image of family.

They were more like the behind-the-scenes Kennedys. The ones who'd been real and human and made mistakes.

"Excuse me," she said, bumping into a man who had stepped out of a building while talking to the man behind him.

She stumbled, he caught her and she smiled her thanks. He smiled back and then she heard someone clear his throat behind him. She glanced over the man's shoulder and straight into the dark chocolate eyes of Inigo Velasquez.

"Inigo!"

She turned on her heel, but she was already a bit off balance and stumbled for one step before straightening her spine and continuing along the sidewalk.

"Have a good one, Marielle," he called after her.

She lifted one hand and gave him the bird as she kept walking. She knew he didn't deserve that from her, but she was just ticked off about him and the situation.

She'd almost gotten him out of her head, and of course she'd see him again. It was kind of like the Marielle law. If she never wanted to see a man again, they'd run into each other. That included her father, Carlton and former lovers.

She finally got to the ad agency for her appointment and stepped into the lobby, moving off to the side to compose herself for a moment.

Was it just her, or did Inigo look even cuter than she remembered? His lips had almost lifted in a smile before tightening. She thought for one second he might have remembered the fun they had before he recalled who she really was.

She took a deep breath. None of that mattered now. She pulled her iPhone from her bag and opened the voice memo that Siobahn had recorded for her. She had made up a song for her to remind Marielle of her new path.

Marielle rules the world,
A badass who makes things happen,
Leaving only smiles in her wake.

She smiled and listened to it two more times. Now the song was in her head. Siobahn had used notes that were designed to stick in the listener's mind. And as she tucked her phone away after checking her lipstick, makeup and hair, she heard the song playing in her mind.

She smiled at the security guard and gave him her ID. He raised one eyebrow at her last name, but it wasn't uncommon, so she just kept smiling as he asked her to put her bag on the scanner and then cleared her to go into the building.

Inigo Velasquez was a memory. A happy memory that she had left behind.

Yeah, right.

Dante Peterson punched Inigo on the arm as Marielle walked away. Both of them were unable to tear their eyes off her. How was it possible she had gotten even more beautiful since he'd last seen her?

She gave him the finger, and he almost smiled before he caught himself. She was his family's enemy. He had to remember that.

"Dude…she doesn't like you," Dante said.

"That's not true. She liked me just fine. I'm the one who doesn't like her," Inigo said.

"Sure you are," he said.

"Screw you, Dante," Inigo said. "She's the other woman. The one Jose was cheating with."

"Well, damn. That really sucks."

"Agreed."

"So how do you know her?" he asked as the Moretti Motors driver pulled up and got out to hold the door to the Vallerio sedan. The car was classy, powerful and the hallmark of the vehicles that Moretti Motors made.

"Where to, Mr. Velasquez?" the driver asked.

"We need to go to the Four Seasons," he informed the driver, sliding into the car first with Dante following behind him.

He really didn't have time to think about Marielle. There were some suspicious things going on with the racing team at Moretti Motors, and Inigo had just left a meeting with the team boss. It was believed that someone on one of the teams was sabotaging his car to ensure that Esteban Acola, the top driver on the Moretti Racing team, would win.

They needed someone with entrée into the high-stakes sports betting world who could infiltrate the operation and do some betting to see if their suspicions were correct. And Inigo was now related through marriage to just such a person. Malcolm Ferris was engaged to Inigo's new sister-in-law's sister, Helena Everton. Malcolm had offered to help out if needed and had arrived in New York last night to meet with Inigo today.

Inigo had brought that information to the meeting.

"I really hope that this turns out to be a false lead. I don't want to think of someone on our team betraying us like that," Inigo said.

"Me either. If it is someone, I'm going to beat the crap out of them," Dante said.

"No, you're not. Marco might, but you're not."

Dante laughed. "You're right. So, about the girl."

"The *woman*. What about her?"

"I know there's more to it than that she was with Jose," he said.

"We hooked up on New Year's, and then the next morning I found out. Bianca confronted her, and she left. That's it. I didn't talk to her again," he said. "I'm kind of pissed at her. I don't believe that she didn't know who we were. She even played all innocent like she was shocked."

"To be fair, she might not have realized who you were. You and Bianca do have different coloring."

"How many brothers-in-law of Jose are drivers? I mean, there's pretty much just me," Inigo reminded his friend.

"Fair enough. So what are you going to do about it?" Dante asked.

What was he going to do about it?

He had no idea. The way she gave him the finger, sort of thumbing her nose at him, had made him want to laugh, but at the same time he remembered the look on Bianca's face New Year's morning. That pain and devastation at seeing the other woman. Sure, his sister was happier now married to

Derek Caruthers than she'd ever been with Jose. But that wound was still there.

Was there something he could do to even the score? To help Bianca heal and maybe get back a bit of his pride? Because a part of him still wasn't sure Marielle hadn't known who he was when she'd slept with him.

"I don't know. It would be sort of fitting if I dated her and then dumped her publicly. She's some sort of social media influencer or something like that. Scarlet mentioned that Marielle was trying to follow in her footsteps."

"Could you do that?" he asked. "I mean, I know hooking up is fine because you know it's just fun and just one night, but dude, you haven't been in a serious relationship since…have you ever been in one?"

Inigo punched his friend on the shoulder. "No. But that's because I never allow anything to interfere with driving. I don't think she'd be any different."

Dante shrugged. "I don't know. I saw the way you watched her."

"Yeah, right. You were too busy staring at her to even notice me," Inigo said. That was another thing about Marielle: she drew attention the way an engine needed fuel. She seemed to enjoy it too. She dressed to impress. He understood from Scarlet and Bianca that clothing, hair and makeup were all tools in the viral social world. He got that. But there was a part of him that couldn't help feeling that she wanted that online life and didn't care what happened off the web.

"True. She's hot," Dante said.

"She is," he said, as the car drew to a stop. They got out and went into Malcolm's hotel. Inigo tucked his idea of revenge away while he waited for Malcolm to answer the door of his suite. But he liked it.

It would give him a chance to get some closure for Bianca and for himself. Because until that moment that they'd seen Bianca and he'd realized who Marielle was, he'd felt…well, that didn't matter. He wasn't a man who got emotionally involved, as Dante had just pointed out. Soon it would be time for him to focus on the upcoming season, and revenge might help him to get Marielle out of his system for good and keep a clear focus going forward.

Malcolm opened the door and invited them in, but there was worry on his face. Inigo wondered if Malcolm was going to be able to do what they were asking of him. He was just getting over his gambling addiction, and asking him to return to that world was a big favor.

Malcolm wanted to impress his fiancée and prove that the past was truly behind him. Facing his demons head-on was one way to prove it. But when Inigo and his friend from Moretti Motors arrived at the hotel suite, he had doubts.

Helena had gone out to have coffee with a college friend, so he'd been waiting for the men alone.

Like all addictions, his sort of flourished when he was by himself. He knew that he could reach out to Mauricio, Inigo's older brother and his best friend, for help, but at the same time he wanted to prove to himself and to his friends and family that he had this. He wasn't going to keep failing.

"Hey, Inigo, great to see you."

"Great to see you too," Inigo said. "This is Dante Peterson, one of the engineers who works on my team. He's going to be monitoring the input to see if there is any tampering."

Malcolm shook hands with both men and led them to the sitting area of the suite, which overlooked Central Park. The room that Moretti Motors had provided for him was impressive and spoke to the money the company had invested in their Formula One racing program, which didn't surprise him. When men were wagering the kind of money that had been talked about, the stakes had to be high.

"So…what is it that they want me to do?" Malcolm asked after he'd offered both men a drink and they'd declined.

"Place some bets. My teammate and I are going to be using the new state-of-the-art indoor racing simulator in secret today. They want to establish a base time before the public practice to confirm their suspicions about sabotage," Inigo said. "If anyone decides to look into your finances, we are going to funnel the money into an account through Hadley to Helena and then you can use it."

"That's fine. I have my own resources, if that would be better," Malcolm said.

"Let me talk to the Moretti Racing team and I'll let you know," Inigo said.

"Fair enough. Should we be meeting and talking like this?" Malcolm asked.

He had wondered about the same thing, but because they were related by marriage, no one thought that it would arise suspicion. "For now, I think it's okay. When you go to place the bet tomorrow, you should say that we are related by marriage and that I was bragging about being really fast this year. Like you sort of have the inside track," Inigo said.

"Are you a braggart?" Malcolm asked.

"He does think the world revolves around him," Dante said.

"Ha. Not really. I mean, I am a good driver, and I'm not going to pretend that winning isn't my focus. And we have put together a plan that is bound to deliver."

"That's all I need. Should we have dinner in public so that the saboteur can see us socializing?" Malcolm asked. He wanted Helena by his side through this process as much as she could be. She was the one who was keeping him strong, and he didn't want to let her down.

"I'll let you know later," Inigo said. "I'll text you."

The two men left a few minutes later, and Malcolm walked around the empty suite. This was why he'd started gambling in the first place, to give Helena the luxe life. He made good money as a Realtor in Cole's Hill, but he wanted her to have this kind of life. And he hadn't wanted to have to wait until they'd been married five or ten years. He wanted to give it to her from the beginning.

Instead he'd lost their savings and almost lost her. He walked to the windows to stare out at the skyline, but all he really saw was himself sleeping in his car and avoiding the love of his life because he had fallen so far down. He hadn't been able to find a way out of it until she'd stepped in and demanded to know what was going on.

He'd told her reluctantly. It had been difficult to lie to Helena. He'd been in love with her since the moment he'd seen her that first day of high school. Sure, he'd known her before that, but when she'd walked into AP US history, he'd really seen her for the first time.

Everyone had said that high school crushes don't last, but there had always been a bond between the two of them. They'd dated and gotten engaged believing the future that they wanted would be easy to achieve. But Helena's family was seriously wealthy—a ranching family that had been in Cole's Hill for a long time. And Malcolm had always known that he was going to have to work extra hard to give her the life—

"I'm back," Helena said, walking into the suite and interrupting his thoughts.

He turned and smiled at her. She wore one of

those knitted hats with a faux fur pom-pom on top. Her cheeks were pink from the cold. She was so beautiful his breath caught in his chest.

She was his. The doubts that had plagued him weren't quieted, but they sort of subsided for a moment. He couldn't lose her. He'd do whatever he had to in order to be the man she needed him to be.

Not an addict who gambled away all of their money, but a man she could be proud to call her own.

"Babe?"

"Yeah?"

"You okay?" she asked, putting her purse on a chair and coming over to him, wrapping her arms around him and resting her head on his chest.

"Yeah. I am now," he said, holding her. He felt the cold that lingered on her jacket and on the tip of her nose when he bent down to kiss her.

Holding her centered him. His addiction sponsor had warned him about turning to another person or thing to replace gambling, but in his heart, he knew that holding Helena and relying on her made him stronger.

And he didn't regret that.

He lifted her into his arms and carried her into the bedroom to make love to her. That always centered him and made him remember why he was staying strong.

Five

"Thank you, Inigo, for coming with me. I really wanted to get a few cute things for the baby while I was here. I'm not sure I'll be coming back to Manhattan for a while after the birth," Bianca said as they left Bonpoint and stepped out into the heavy foot traffic on Madison Avenue.

He held his four-year-old nephew Benito's hand and all of his sister's bags as they walked up the street. On a certain level, this shopping trip was his way of apologizing for sleeping with Marielle. He'd never meant to hurt his sister, and he knew that seeing Jose's former mistress on New Year's Day had upset her.

"Not a problem. I love spending time with you and Benito."

"Me too, *Tío*," Benito said. He was holding a small wooden replica of the first Moretti Motors Formula One car.

"But you hate shopping," she said. "Don't deny it. No man wants to spend hours looking at children's clothing."

"Honestly, it was a nice distraction this morning. I have my first time trial in the new simulator, and I would have just been going over setups and running the track in my head if I hadn't come with you. And I pretty much did that last night, so we're good."

She laughed. "I'd forgotten what it was like to be in that life. Jose was like that, always thinking about the tracks and the setup. He'd wake up in the middle of the night and jot down notes for his engineers or sometimes even call them," she said.

There was a note in her voice that he didn't recognize, but he did know this was the first time that he'd heard Bianca talk about her deceased husband without a layer of bitterness. "He was very demanding. But that was what made him the best."

"Was it?" she asked.

He glanced down at Benito, who wasn't paying them the least bit of attention. "What else would it be?"

"I don't know. Maybe the lifestyle, the women, the attention from the paparazzi—you know how he ate that up."

Jose had been the kind of person who commanded attention wherever he went, not unlike a movie star or a famous rock and roll singer. There had been something about him that just drew every eye in the room. Inigo hadn't been surprised that women were drawn to him; he knew men were too. He'd been charming and funny and had a way of making each person he spoke to feel as if they were the only one who mattered.

But Inigo had been surprised that Jose hadn't been loyal to Bianca. How had he read that wrong? There had been a feeling of sincerity in his brother-in-law that Inigo still couldn't mesh with the reality of what he'd learned after Jose's death.

"He did," Inigo said at last. "Do you want to talk about her?"

"No. I never want to discuss that. You know she wasn't the only one," Bianca said. "Just the last one."

He had known that. He'd learned it from his tech-genius brother, Alec, who had dug deep on the internet to find all of the details so that there would be no more surprises for their sister. He got all the dirt that Jose had hidden from them and laid it bare. There would be no more surprises from beyond the grave.

"He was such a bastard," Inigo said but then shook his head. Jose hadn't been, though. For all his faults, he'd come across as a great guy.

"It would have been easier if he had been," Bianca said.

As they continued up Madison nearing the famous Ralph's Coffee that was part of the flagship Ralph Lauren store, he could see a crowd of people. "I wonder what that is."

"Me too," Bianca said. "I love the energy in the city. It's so different from Cole's Hill."

"Definitely. At home the only crowds are at the Bull Pen on Friday night."

"So true," she said. "Can you see who it is? I wonder if it's someone famous."

Inigo maneuvered around people trying to get a glimpse of the person and stopped in his tracks as he saw the familiar long silver-shot blond hair and silvery-gray eyes. Marielle.

"It's no one famous," he said.

"Oh, it's probably just someone you don't recognize. Maybe a Kardashian."

"It's not. I know who they are," Inigo said, trying to steer Bianca away from the crowd. But his sister was stubborn and elbowed him.

"Stop it, Inigo. You're being silly. I want to see who it is," she said, moving closer.

He wasn't going to physically keep her from seeing Marielle. After all, she was pregnant and needed to be careful. But his sister had definitely inherited their mother's mule headedness.

She made her way forward, and the crowd shifted. He knew the instant his sister saw her. Her back stiffened, and she turned away, walking back toward him. "You did know who it was."

"I did. I wasn't sure…"

"Don't worry. I think I've had enough of the city. Can you get me a cab?" she said, reaching over and taking Benito's hand.

He nodded and lifted his arm to hail a cab. Two women walked by them as he did so.

"I love her. She's got the best life and advice. I want to be Mari when I grow up. She's really got it together."

His eyes met his sister's, and he saw the color drain from her face.

"Bia—"

"Don't. Please don't say anything. I hate that she's Insta-famous and that people want to be like her," Bianca said. The cab pulled up, and he opened the door. He helped Benito into the back seat first and then turned to hug his sister. She seemed smaller now, less in command, and he hated that.

He felt someone watching him and looked up to see that Marielle had noticed them. She lifted her hand to her lips and blew them a kiss. She had no shame. Not a shred of remorse over what she had done to Bianca.

Marielle was very pleased with the meeting she'd had. She tried not to look smug as she left the building on Fifth Avenue, but it was hard. The day was cold and gray, and after the way her new year had started, she had felt the same. But she was shaking it off. She decided to stop by Ralph's for coffee.

She posed in front of the famous Ralph's sign for

a selfie and shared it with her followers with a tease that she had big news coming before going inside. A few of her followers spotted her and came over to pose with her and to chat. She was enjoying the moment a lot; this was something she'd never thought she'd find for herself. She texted Scarlet to thank her for recommending her for the meeting and then her manager to make sure he knew the terms she'd negotiated with the brand.

She glanced up to see Inigo and his sister staring at her. Jose's son was with them, but he was engrossed in the toy in his hand. Bianca turned away, and Inigo followed her to hail a cab. Marielle felt some of her happiness ebb away, and as Inigo hugged his sister and looked at her, she realized part of what she felt was guilt—but also defiance. So she lifted her hand and blew them a kiss before turning and walking away.

Coffee would cure all of her problems, she thought as she joined the line in Ralph's. A moment later someone entered the shop and got in line behind her.

"I'd ask if you are following me, but you were here first," Inigo said from behind her.

She turned around and looked into chocolaty-brown eyes. He stood there looking better than he had a right to. "Shouldn't you be in Europe training for the upcoming season?"

"Nope. Moretti Racing built a new facility on Long Island and we're using it for the preseason training. They're trying to get a foothold in the US market and nab up-and-coming drivers before they commit to NASCAR."

"Just my luck," she said.

"You say that like I did something to you," he said. "I'm not the one at fault here."

She shook her head. "Gentlemanly of you to point that out."

She gave the barista her order, paid and then stepped away from Inigo. Why had she even bothered to speak to him? She should have ignored him.

But how could she?

She wanted him to accuse her of being a homewrecker so she could defend herself. Tell him how Jose had said he was divorced. How Jose had made it sound like he was the victim. But really, what would that help? She'd been seeing a married man. The fact that she'd thought he was divorced didn't really matter, did it?

Carlton had told her to stay away from married men when he'd stepped in to fix the PR nightmare she'd created. And her father had backed up Carlton's warning with a solid disinheritance threat if she didn't toe the line.

Inigo stepped over to her, and she rolled her eyes as he arched one eyebrow at her. "Would you like to join me?"

"Why?" she asked.

"So we can say goodbye properly. We never had the chance," he said.

She thought about it for a minute. He was right.

If they ended this the way they should have on New Year's Day, then maybe she'd be able to forget him and move on. She was of course already moving on, but the part of her that kept thinking that she didn't have to would get the hint.

"Sure," she said.

"Why don't you grab us a table and I'll get our drinks," he suggested.

"Sounds good," she said, scanning the seating area for a free table. When she spotted one, she moved quickly to grab it. She sat down and took an antibacterial wipe from her handbag and cleaned the table.

Inigo set their drinks on the table before sitting down across from her. He stretched his legs out under the table, brushing against hers. She shifted around, crossing her feet under the chair so he wasn't touching her.

She wasn't doing this again. She couldn't. She'd hooked up with him once, and that was okay, but now…knowing who he was? Nah, she didn't need that kind of trouble in her life.

"So…" she said. She'd never been good at leaving something alone. If she had a scab, she picked at it. Not that she was saying that Inigo was like a scab, but the way he made her feel was similar. Her skin felt too tight when she was around him. Like she had an itch that couldn't be scratched. Part of it was sexual, but a bigger part was just the mélange of emotions he stirred in her.

"So, you and Jose, huh?" he asked.

She put her arms on the table, holding her coffee cup loosely in her hands. Of course they were going to have to talk about Jose. "Yeah. Do you really want to discuss that?"

He turned away from her and she noticed he had a strong jaw, especially when he clenched it. "No. I don't. I just don't get it."

"What's to get? He was funny and charming. He told me his marriage was over," she said. "I believed him."

"He was funny," Inigo agreed, ignoring the rest. She really didn't blame him.

"Yeah. How well did you know him?"

"He was my mentor. I started racing karts when I was thirteen. The next year he started dating Bianca, and he sort of took me under his wing. I thought… well, it doesn't matter, but his death was hard on me. Then after he died, I learned about the thing with you. It was like losing him again," Inigo admitted.

She could tell he hadn't meant to tell her that last bit. But it really drove home the fact that the two of them shouldn't be doing this. She wanted closure and not friendship, yet his pain mirrored her own. She had been betrayed by Jose as well—not that Inigo would see it that way. But the truth was she'd had an expectation that Jose was an honest man.

"I'm sorry. I miss the fun person I knew. Not the other guy that I learned he was later," she said.

She put her hand on Inigo's where it was clenched

on the table. He looked over at her, and she couldn't read the expression in his eyes. That troubled her. Had she said the wrong thing? Hell, when didn't she?

"I'm sorry too," he said. "I wish you hadn't known him."

"I'm not," she said. Without Jose she would never had gotten the wake-up call she needed to figure out what she wanted for her life instead of following the script of what everyone expected her to do.

Her response surprised him. He thought she'd have said she wished she hadn't been the other woman, but she seemed pretty okay with it to him. The idea of revenge stirred again in the back of his mind. He thought back on his sister's pale face, which served as a strong reminder of how much Marielle had hurt her. He wanted to think he wasn't petty and base, but every time he tried to be the better man, it came back. He didn't need the distraction, which Dante had been quick to point out, yet at the same time, when would he have a chance for payback like this again?

"I'm surprised. I'd think being with a married man—"

"It wasn't like that. You more than anyone know how it is on the road during the season. I was a cup girl. I was traveling around with the teams, and we met. There are the drivers who don't have sex at all, and then the others who are always looking to get laid."

She was so blunt. Her words were the truth. He'd seen it himself as he walked through the trailers. He was aware of the women with hot passes waiting to see who was looking to get lucky. Some of the drivers even believed if they had sex right before a race it improved their performance behind the wheel. Esteban was one of those men. It definitely hadn't hurt him behind the wheel.

"I guess the lives of the families back home don't matter," he said glibly. Why had he sat down with her?

A part of him wanted to believe she was more than she seemed. More than Bia had made her out to be. He couldn't help remembering their night together in the O'Malleys' guesthouse. It had been special.

"It's a different world. You know it doesn't feel like real life," she said.

"Hmm. That's interesting. For me it's where I'm most at home and more myself than anywhere else," he said.

"You would say that. You're a driver. You probably don't feel alive unless you're going three hundred miles per hour. You're not human like the rest of us."

"Not human?"

"You know, you're like a demigod moving that fast. Not paying attention to anything that gets caught under your tires and blown toward the side of the road."

"You don't know me," he said. "Some drivers might be that way, but I'm not."

She shrugged, taking a sip of her coffee. He noticed her lipstick left a mark on the side of the cup. She was like that mark on the cup, but on his psyche. Their one night together was bright red.

Had it been a fluke? He wished he could easily figure that out. If it was, then he could walk away. Should he try it again? What the hell?

He wondered if it was the lack of sleep or just his nerves at the thought that someone might be working to actively keep him from winning. Or if it was her crystal-gray eyes watching him like a dare. Causing him to stop weighing the consequences and teasing him into taking what he wanted.

And he did want her.

But then he thought of that smug look on her face when she'd said that during the racing season regular rules of decency didn't apply. It wasn't that he normally gave a crap about how people behaved unless it affected him, but she'd hurt Bia. That kind of thinking had been responsible for hurting his sister.

He couldn't let her get away with it. She might find someone else to hurt by her actions. He wasn't holding himself up as some sort of moral police—he knew he had flaws—but he couldn't just walk away after she'd said that. She wasn't even taking responsibility for her own culpability in the affair. She'd pretty much said that since drivers have big egos, it was Jose's fault.

He wasn't letting Jose off the hook, but he was dead, so there wasn't much that Inigo could do about that.

"I don't know you," she said. "I did sort of like you, though."

"Did?" he asked. If he was going to make this work, he had to let go of showing her he was pissed and at least try to be charming. The only thing was, when he tried to be, he never could pull it off.

"Well, you haven't been very nice today," she said.

"You gave me the finger," he said. He could still picture her hand in the air as she walked away from him.

"You thought it was funny, didn't you?" she asked.

He had. "I don't know what to do with you."

She tipped her head to the side, and her long blond hair flowed over one shoulder. She pouted at him with those full lips for a second and then said, "You did okay when we were in the bedroom."

Immediately he felt a jolt go through him. "We got along pretty good, didn't we?"

"Uh-huh. Was it just a one-night hookup? I mean, before you found out about the thing with your sister, did you think we'd see each other again?"

Wow. That was the million-dollar question. If he said no, he'd come off like a douche, and if he said yes, he'd seem like a sap who had placed an emotional price on their night together.

"I don't know," he answered as honestly as he could. "I liked you, and I wasn't ready to think about more than spending the day with you."

"Fair enough. So, are we going somewhere from here? Or is it so long?" she asked.

"You're very blunt," he said.

"I am. It's just that when I expect things, they never turn out like I think they should. If I ask and still get disappointed, I've got no one to blame but myself."

Six

Marielle had always lived her life in the nothing ventured, nothing gained mind-set. Scarlet's late sister, Ivy, used to call it the "leap and end up with scratched knees" motto. Either way, Marielle wasn't one to hedge her bets. More than once it had netted her something she hadn't expected. And she couldn't regret that. One of the things that she'd been running from when she'd left home to be a trophy girl in the F1 was her safe, boring life. Though her mom seemed happy with her life as Mrs. Bisset, Marielle had wanted more. Or at least some adventure before she became a Mrs.

"Blame is a tricky thing," he said. "It always seems to imply regret to me."

She smiled and couldn't help it. She wanted to make him out to be just like Jose and the other drivers she'd met during her year on the F1 circuit, but he was different. It wasn't just the way he made her feel like she was going to explode if she didn't touch him. Or the way he made her wish she could just drown in his deep brown gaze for an afternoon. It was something more. She'd venture to say that he got her, that he understood where she was coming from. But she couldn't be certain of that yet.

"Do you have many regrets, speedy?"

He shook his head. "Nope. I always go full out, and if it doesn't work out…well, then, at least I tried."

"Me too," she said.

He shook his head. "I don't want to like you."

"Well, there you have it."

She shouldn't have been surprised that his words hurt her a little, but she was. She knew that she was persona non grata in his eyes. That she'd crossed a line that most decent people thought shouldn't be crossed. But at the same time, she had just felt like he got her. Apparently, she was wrong.

Shocker. *Not!*

She pushed her chair back and started to stand up, but he caught her hand in his. "I'm sorry. That was an asshole thing to say."

"It was."

"The thing is, I do like you. You keep surprising me, and I know that I shouldn't be sitting here with you, but I am. And I don't want you to walk away angry."

She tugged her hand from his. She got what he was saying. But this was complicated. And honestly, not the kind of thing she needed right now. It had been fun to flirt with him and pretend that coffee could lead to something more, but this was Inigo Velasquez. The brother-in-law of Jose Ruiz. She'd made herself a promise when that relationship had ended.

No more Formula One drivers. No more men who were so used to moving through life at blinding speed. No more.

So why was she lingering?

She should grab her bag and walk out of here with a haughty toss of her head.

Instead she was looking into those big brown eyes and searching for something that she knew she wasn't going to find. That she had told herself she didn't need and that she could live without.

"Let me buy you dinner to apologize."

"Hmm…let me think about it," she said. She reached into her bag and pulled out one of her business cards and handed it to him. Then she grabbed a second one. "Here's my contact information. Write yours on here."

She handed him the extra card and a pen and watched as he wrote in a hasty scrawl. He passed the card back to her, and she tucked it into her coat pocket before smiling at him and turning away.

She zipped up her coat as she walked through the busy coffeehouse to the door. She told herself she wasn't going to look back, but when she walked by the tables, she couldn't help herself. He was staring down at the card with her contact details on it. She shook her head, thinking she didn't understand him at all.

She hailed a cab and gave them her brother's brownstone address without a second thought. She needed someone to talk sense to her. Girlfriends were good for telling her what she wanted to hear, but Darian would tell her the truth whether it hurt or not. He'd always been good about that.

She got out at his Upper East Side address, then hurried past people on the sidewalk and up the stairs to let herself in. As soon as she did, Bailey came to greet her.

The large St. Bernard came barreling at her, barking his hello. She braced herself as he went up on his back legs to greet her, licking her chin as she turned her head.

"That's what you get for not knocking," Darian said.

"Sorry, Dare. I was afraid you might be out back staring at a cigarette and wouldn't let me in," she said, rubbing Bailey behind his ears until the dog was satisfied and trotted back down the hall to his master.

"When you come out swinging, I know you're not sure of something," he said.

"When am I ever sure?" she asked. "Please tell me that one day I will not be this big hot mess."

"Mom seems to think so," he said. "But so far I haven't seen anyone who has it together."

"Not even you, big bro? You're a political strategist. You look good on paper and you know how to make everyone else look good too," she said.

"All of the Bissets look good, Mare. So, what's up?" he asked, leading the way into his den. She could tell he'd been working, because he had a can of Red Bull next to his laptop. He gestured for her to sit down on the leather couch and when she did, he sat next to her.

"Uh, um, I ran into Inigo Velasquez again. We exchanged some words, and he invited me to dinner. I know I shouldn't go," she said.

Then she looked at her older brother, who leaned back, crossing his arms over his chest. "I shouldn't, right?"

"Tell me everything," he invited.

She did, pouring it all out. The stuff about Bianca and how it had made her feel like pond scum, but how she'd responded by blowing them a kiss, which made Dare wince. She told him about liking Inigo, giving him the bird, having coffee and getting lost in his eyes.

"Mare, I don't know how you do it, but God knows you could make walking across the street into something complicated," he said at last.

"I know. What should I do?" she asked him.

He considered it for a while, and she got fidgety. The fact that she had come and asked for advice was probably all the indication she needed that she shouldn't go out with Inigo.

"Go. You'll regret it if you don't."

"I might regret it if I do," she said.

"Well, then, you might as well give yourself something to regret," he said.

Getting into the simulator and putting on his helmet at the Moretti Racing facility forced Inigo to remember what was at stake. Last night he'd been drinking ice water and using the Peloton in the house he'd rented that was only a few miles from the facility. He'd been thinking about the text message he didn't receive from Marielle.

But that was a distraction.

Revenge.

Who did he think he was? Machiavelli?

Marco Moretti was in town. Right now, he was standing in the booth next to Keke Heckler. Both men were legendary drivers and had built the Moretti Racing program from the ground up. Inigo had been ecstatic when they'd asked him to be a part of the team three years ago. And they'd taken him from middle-of-the-pack finishes to the top ten. But he craved the championship.

There was no room for revenge in a winning driver's psyche. He knew that. Dante had been funny in the car, but the truth was his friend and head engineer for his team had a point. He should only do things that improved his time and his racing.

"How does the cockpit feel?" Marco asked. He spoke very good English, but the hint of his Italian upbringing was there in every word.

"Good," Inigo said, adjusting his shoulder straps. The cockpit he was sitting in mirrored the custom-made interior of his actual car. The seat had been molded to fit his body and had been placed at the exact length from the steering wheel and pedals that he liked. He twisted his head and shoulders, popping his neck before he settled into the seat.

They were running the Melbourne course, which would be the first race of the season. He closed his eyes and reached through all of his memories to the Melbourne race last year. He remembered the atmosphere and the people. The weather and the day. He wanted to be in the right mind-set.

"I'm ready," he said.

"Good. We're set up too," Dante said.

The simulation had him on a qualifying lap, so he waited, watched the lights, and when they hit green, he hit the gas. When he drove, there wasn't time for anything else except the track. He didn't think when he drove—he reacted. He became one with the car and drove like the machine was an extension of his body.

He pushed everything from his mind but couldn't help remembering the feel of his hands on the curves of Marielle's hips. The car reacted the same way she had, responding to his every touch. He continued the course, coming up on the finish line as everything in him was narrowing down to the track, the touch, the sound of the engine. That first lap time would be recorded, and he kept driving knowing they wanted the best of three and would get an average.

The team of engineers who worked on his car were recording every detail. There was even someone who was monitoring his heart rate to see if it increased as he powered through the turns.

"Good time. Take a break and we'll set up for another run," Dante said through the speakers. "The team noticed a slight hesitation in the engine. We want to tweak that."

"Okay," Inigo said, getting out of the simulator. He walked over to the area where Marco and Keke stood.

"I like what I'm seeing," Marco said. "I have a good feeling about this year for you."

"Me too," he admitted to his boss.

Keke rubbed the back of his neck. His once blond hair was now streaked with gray, but the forty-seven-year-old former driver was still fit and sharp. "You're all in for training, right? No outside distractions?"

He nodded. Where was Keke going with this? "Always. I don't drink, work out and try to keep my focus on the track."

"Good. That's really good. I hate to bring this up," Keke said.

"Why?" Marco asked. "If you have a concern, you should mention it."

"I am mentioning it," Keke said. The men had been teammates and were good friends—at times the dynamic reminded Inigo of his relationship with his brothers or Dante.

Keke turned to him. "My wife mentioned she heard a rumor that you were linked with the up-and-coming lifestyle guru Mari."

"Damn," Marco said, looking at Inigo. "I wanted to rib him about turning into an old woman, but is that true? You've always been about no women during the season."

Keke's wife was the former swimsuit model Elena Hamilton. Elena had turned to designing swimsuits after her modelling career had ended and was one of the top designers for athletes now.

"It's…it's sort of true. We hooked up on New Year's Eve," he said. "I don't see it going anywhere."

Especially since she hadn't texted him back about dinner. Was he thinking about that, about being stood up, and not about the revenge plan he had for her? Not very Machiavellian of him, was it?

"Good. I don't know her," Keke said. "But wasn't there something with her and a driver where she was the trophy girl?"

"Woman," Inigo said.

"What?" Keke asked.

"Women don't like to be called girls," Inigo said. "She was a trophy woman."

Marco started laughing. "Good luck with that. Elena and my wife, Virginia, have been trying to bring him into the twenty-first century."

"Hey, I didn't mean any disrespect," Keke said.

"I know," Inigo said. "Force of habit."

"Fair enough. You know I don't give a crap about your personal life, so if you want to date or hook up with a different *woman* before every race, that's up to you. Just make sure it enhances your racing profile. You are sharper this year, and we think you could win races and actually be in contention for the championship."

He heard what Keke was saying. He had nothing but respect for both him and Marco. These two knew what it was like to race and win, and Inigo wanted that. But he also wanted to make Marielle pay for how she'd made Bianca feel. "I will. Nothing is more important to me than winning."

"That's what we like to hear," Marco said.

Dante and his team finished up on the simulator, and Inigo got back in to take another test run. This time he pushed the thought of Marielle further out of his mind and concentrated on the track. On beating his previous time. And he did it.

Marielle saw the call from her mom and hit Ignore. She had a feeling that Darian might have let slip some of the details of what was going on in her life. Normally her mom wasn't the touchy-feely type, but she'd called every day for the last week. The family usually communicated through a chat app with Carlton, who kept everyone's calendars. So she knew it wasn't an emergency.

And she didn't want to talk to her mom. All of her life Marielle had been struggling to get out from under her mother's shadow. She'd been the perfect hostess and wife. Everyone always wanted to talk to Marielle about her mom and her mom's style. She looked effortlessly chic, and Marielle's own manager had more than once suggested she could grow her followers more easily if she'd just embrace the classic Bisset style, but she didn't want that.

Who wanted to feel like the only reason they were successful was because of their mom? Not her. But more than that, she and her mother hadn't ever really gotten along. Marielle was pretty sure that was due to the fact that her mom didn't like to share attention from the men in the family. Or at least that's what her psychiatrist had hinted at.

She didn't know. But when her mother called again five minutes after the last call, Marielle answered.

"Hey."

"Hello, Marielle," her mother said. Her mother had gone to a boarding school in Switzerland and had retained a somewhat understated European accent despite the fact that she'd been living in the United States for the last thirty years.

"What's up?"

"Straight to the point as always," her mom said.

"I heard through a friend that you're becoming a very popular influencer. Your name showed up on a list of those I should invite for the Bridgehampton Winter Classic."

"Wow. That's great news," she said. "Of course, I'll come."

"The odd thing is that you aren't on there as Marielle Bisset, you are listed Mari-Marielle Alexandria."

"I know. I didn't want anyone to think I was representing our family," she said. "You've mentioned a number of times that I'm not always great at that."

She heard her mother sigh. "That's only the truth. Even Carlton agrees."

"I know," she said. He'd told her on many occasions.

"Aside from that…how are we going to handle this? Do you want me to pretend I don't know you?"

She hadn't thought that far ahead when she'd started her account. "No. I think people who have known us both for years will think that's silly. I won't publicize it on my account. Do you think that would work?"

"I don't know, Marielle. This is very odd. Let me discuss it with your father and Carlton, and I'll get back to you. For right now I'm going to put you down as a maybe on the list."

"Mom, this is a huge event for influencers. It would hurt my career not to be there," she said.

"I'll take that under consideration," she said. "I'll let you know later today."

Marielle hit the disconnect button before she said something she'd regret later and slammed the phone down on the table in front of her. She couldn't deal with this. All of her life she'd been struggling to find a way to be the woman she wanted to be and now that she was so close, her name was once again standing in her way.

She so wished she'd been born Marielle Smith or Jones or anything other than Bisset.

Her phone buzzed, and she saw it was a group message from Carlton requesting a family meeting to discuss "the M problem."

"The M problem?" she said out loud to her apartment. Of course they'd need a meeting for that.

She texted back she was out of the country. And she intended to be.

Her phone rang a minute later. *Darian.*

"Mar, what is going on?"

"Mom found out that I'm doing the social media influencer thing and doesn't know if I should be invited to events she's on the committee for. She actually asked if she should pretend not to know me."

"Oh, that's—"

"Messed up. But hey, it's me," she said.

"I'm not going to allow this. I'm going to speak to Dad about it," Darian said. "You know if you went to him, she'd have to back off."

"I do know that. But I also know that if I do, she'll be a total witch to me every time I see her," Marielle said. "I'm just not sure how to play this."

"Don't play it. Come to the meeting and just say this is what you are doing. It'd be ridiculous not to associate with you regardless of the name you use," Darian said. "I know that our brothers will agree with me."

"Zac definitely will, but he's training for the America's Cup and doesn't mind ruffling feathers because he's not around to suffer the consequences. Logan might feel differently since he has to see Dad every day. And who knows what Leo will say?"

"Trust me," Darian said. "I'll talk to them and we'll present a united front. Come to my place tomorrow night at six. I'll have it all worked out."

"Aren't you supposed to be working on some big campaign strategy?" she asked, loving her big brother for stepping in but knowing she shouldn't rely on him to do this for her.

"I can do both, kiddo. Just be here tomorrow night."

"I will be," she said. "Love you, Dare."

"Love you, too."

She hung up with her brother, and a moment later he responded in the group text that they were all unavailable. Immediately her sibling chat group lit up with her other brothers wanting to know what was going on. Darian just said he'd explain everything at six at his place. Zac said that he would join by video chat, but it was cutting into his training time.

It had always struck her how odd it was that all of the Bisset siblings spent more time away from their parents than with them. Even though Mari had been crashing at their family home in East Hampton, she'd made sure to arrange it so she wouldn't have to spend too much time with her folks.

Seven

Marielle still hadn't texted Inigo back. Instead she was hanging with her bestie, Siobahn Murphy. Siobahn had been the lead singer for Venus Rising since she was fourteen. The band had been comprised of older members and they'd been put together by a producer who...was no longer with the band. Marielle and Siobahn had met at a party at the Royal Bahamas club when they were both eighteen. They'd been young, had too much money and both of them had a simple goal: live life to the fullest. For Marielle she'd just wanted to not be like her parents and her older brothers. It wasn't much of a goal, but it had worked.

Looking at both of them now, eight years later, it seemed that life had certainly not worked out the way either of them planned. Siobahn was fresh off a breakup; her ex, a singer-songwriter, had immediately eloped to Vegas with one of her dancers. It had almost broken Siobahn, who had truly loved Mate.

Sitting in Marielle's apartment eating vegan pizza on a Friday night wasn't what they had envisioned for themselves at twenty-six. They should be owning it. But sometimes Marielle thought this was owning it.

Her mom hadn't tried to speak to her again after Darian had sent his last message to the group chat and Marielle was relieved but also a little sad. Would it kill her mom to act maternal to her for once?

"Ugh. I don't really like this cauliflower pizza crust," Siobahn said. "Just got an invite to the Polar club. Want to check it out?"

"Yes. I was just thinking we should be out on a Friday night… I need to meet someone and hook up so I can wash away my last one," Marielle said. She wouldn't have admitted that to anyone other than Siobahn, but her friend understood.

"Me too. Mate is posting pictures of him and the wife on his yacht. Last year that was me. And I hate that I still care, but…"

"Let's go. We're going to find some hot guys, hook up, and then we'll both be in a better state of mind," Marielle said.

"Let's do it," Siobahn said, following her into her bedroom, which had a huge walk-in closet that Marielle had spent a year designing and having built.

She'd sort of retreated to her apartment and spent

a lot of time redoing it. That was how she started her social media channel, just working on the apartment and working through her issues at the same time.

They raided her closet and both came away with outfits that suited them. Then she called down to her driver, Stevens. Technically he was Darian's driver, but Dare hardly ever used him. Her brother liked to walk so he could eavesdrop on conversations and hear what was really on people's minds. He used that information when plotting strategy for his clients. He really was too good for this world, she thought, not for the first time.

He could be tough when he had to, but he always put everyone else first. *Especially her.* She needed to figure out how to deal with her mom without involving him.

Someday.

"Girl, we are going to own it tonight," Siobahn said as she snapped a selfie of the two of them.

Twenty minutes later, seated in the VIP section of Polar, Marielle wasn't too sure her plan for the evening was the best one. Sure, there were a lot of guys who seemed to be willing to hook up with her, but she just felt…they weren't doing it for her. She couldn't help comparing each man to Inigo. She wasn't trying to, but she'd notice that one's jaw wasn't as strong as his was. That another one's eyes weren't as warm and chocolaty. That yet another suitor didn't smile at her smart-ass comments the way Inigo did.

He wasn't the man for her. She knew this. So why was every guy not as good as him?

That ticked her off. She was headed to the bar to get a couple of shots of tequila, which always made even the most mediocre of evenings better, when she heard a familiar Texan drawl. She stopped and glanced around, and there he was. The very man she'd come here to forget—and failed.

Was it karma?

She'd decided to move on and couldn't because… they weren't done with each other, she thought. He glanced over in her direction, and their gazes met. His face tightened for a moment, and then he shook his head.

He lifted his hand and crooked his finger at her, and she stood there and started laughing. It didn't matter that they weren't perfect for each other. That the world was never going to be a place where they could be a couple because of her past actions. He got her.

She walked toward him, and he moved away from the high table where he'd been toward her.

"How is it that the one woman I'm trying to forget I keep bumping into?" he asked.

"Karma. I've just decided it's karma. I'm not sure if it's good or bad or what," she admitted.

"Karma, eh? Sure, I'll go with that," he said. "I promised myself I wasn't going to sleep with you again, but you look so damn hot in that…is that even a dress?"

"Of course it is," she said. They were both trying so hard to avoid fate, she thought, but there was no way they were going to be successful.

"Dance with me, Inigo. Let me put my hands all over you and we can pretend that it will be enough until midnight, when we both have to leave and go home to our real lives."

"Is that what you said to Jose?" he asked.

And it was like a knife right in her heart. "No, it's not."

Surprised at how deeply that had hurt, she turned and walked away from him. She was used to jabs from the media, from her mom, but Inigo had surprised her. He definitely didn't get her if he could say something like that to her.

Inigo almost let her go, but he wasn't an asshole—as much as that comment had made him sound and feel like one. The thing with Jose was harder to shake than he wanted to admit. And he was in the club trying to forget Marielle, but then there she was.

He had to force his way through the crowd to her. She was seated in the VIP area, but luckily the club's owner was an F1 fan and the bouncer knew him. The man lifted the rope and let Inigo through, but as he got closer and saw her face, he knew he should just apologize and leave.

His thoughts of revenge were a distant memory at this point because he'd never witnessed the aftermath of his senseless tongue before, and he definitely didn't like what he saw.

Her friend noticed him before Marielle did and came at him with attitude and probably more than a bit of violence on her mind.

"I'm a total d-bag. I know it," he said as she approached. He recognized her as the singer Siobahn Murphy, not just because everyone knew who she was but also because she'd been in Cole's Hill for a month with Scarlet a few months ago. His sister liked her.

"You really are. Wait, aren't you Bianca's little brother?"

"I am."

"I guess it's safe to say that every family has assholes," she said.

He started to argue, but she interrupted him.

"Don't. I know you're mad, and you might feel slightly bad about what you did to her, but she deserves better. No one is perfect—you might want to remember that."

"I know that better than most. Listen, I shouldn't have said it, and I need to apologize, but not to you. So, either sit down or go and do your thing."

Siobahn raised her eyebrows at him. "You've got five minutes and then I'm intervening, and trust me you aren't going to like that."

Siobahn walked past him, and Inigo realized that while he and Siobahn had been talking Marielle had composed herself. She looked bored and beautiful, but he felt like maybe he could still see the hurt in her eyes. That she wasn't really ready to talk to him.

But this wasn't something that he could let go.

"I'm sorry," he said as he approached her booth and slid onto the bench across from her. "I have no excuse except that I guess it bothers me that I want you so much when I know that I can't have you."

She didn't say a word, just shook her head. And he guessed he didn't deserve anything more than that.

"The truth is—"

"I don't care," she interrupted. "I thought you were someone…that doesn't matter now. Fine, I heard your apology and I accept it. You can leave now."

Leave now.

He should do just that. He'd seen what happened when he hurt her, but she had been quick to move on. Would he even be able to make her feel bad if he dated her and broke up with her in a public way? Also, could he stop himself from falling for her? It was harder than he had imagined. There was something about her…

He'd told himself there was no way he could be with her and that wasn't just talk to keep himself from getting involved during the racing season. He legitimately couldn't be with her.

But he'd hurt her, and he hated himself for that. He'd meant to remind himself that she couldn't be his, and probably he'd sealed his fate. Ensured she'd never look at him with that heady cocktail of lust and affection again.

"I could. But I… I can't. I just don't want to leave it like this. Every time I try to fix this, I seem to be making it worse. And believe me when I say that's not how I normally operate."

She almost smiled. He saw her lips twitch. Aware that the clock was running before her friend came back and kicked him out of Marielle's life, he knew the next few seconds were very important. But his whole life was measured in seconds. In making snap decisions and trusting his instincts. He felt time warp around him the way it did when he was driving. He knew that whatever he did next would decide if he spent more time with this woman or lived with regret the rest of his life.

His pulse was racing, but he felt calm. He was in his element, and unlike earlier, when he'd been riding hormones, he was ready for this.

"I want to believe you, but you keep letting me down," she said.

"I feel like I know the answer to this. But will you give me one more chance to prove I'm not that guy?" he asked.

She chewed on her lower lip, and it was the first thing he'd seen her do that revealed her nerves. Even the night they'd met, she'd been cool and composed. It was the first time he saw that she was real. That underneath the sassy comebacks and quick smiles there was a hell of a lot more going on. He had to fix this and leave, he thought.

"Until midnight," he said.

That was his last offer. He liked her on a level that made no rational sense to him. She was a distraction, the last woman he should be chatting up, but at the same time, he couldn't just walk away.

"Dance with me," he said. "One dance, and if you still don't want to give me another second, I'm out."

"Dance with you? Isn't that what I suggested?"

"It is, which is why I'm hoping you have an interest in either forgiveness or humiliating me on the dance floor."

She shook her head. "I'm not like that."

"Give me a chance to get to know you. I'll stop saying dumb things…well, maybe that's too big of an ask, but I'll try to stop."

She laughed, and he felt it all the way to his core. His racing vision left, and he was once again just a man sitting across from a gorgeous woman, knowing that if she said yes, he was one lucky bastard and he should work hard to not screw up anything else this evening.

"Yes."

Marielle felt like she'd had too much to drink. She knew she shouldn't be dancing with him, not now. Not after what he'd said. He'd shown her who he really was, and she had to remember that. But it was too bad that her hormones hadn't gotten the message. She was still attracted to him. He had a sweet smile that was sensual at the same time. It was his mouth. That damned perfectly formed mouth of his that had made her say yes.

Now she was swaying to the music under the strobe lights of the club, pressed close to him because of the crowd on the dance floor. The energy was electric, and she felt it pulsing through every inch of her. Inigo must too, she thought. He had his hand on her hip, and he undulated against her. He knew how to move.

She was trying to remember that he said stupid things, but honestly at this moment all she could think about was getting him alone and getting him naked again.

A part of her acknowledged that she wanted to walk away with the upper hand this time, not be the one left shattered by the morning after, but another part didn't give a damn about any of that. She was hot and horny, and she wanted this man. Inigo was the only one who could satisfy her tonight, and after a long week where she definitely had more lows than highs, she was going to take what she wanted.

The music changed to an old Pitbull club song, and Inigo jumped in the air pumping his fist. He leaned over, wrapping his arm around her, pulling her into the curve of his body. "I love this song."

She could tell. The beat was sensual and hot, Cuban beats with the Miami heat, and Inigo moved to the music like it was flowing through him. His hands were soft on her hips, urging her to find the same movements as he had. She stopped thinking, stopped analyzing and let the music consume her the way that it had Inigo. She sank deeper into the curve of his body. She felt his hips against hers and his hands sliding up and down her sides. She felt the ridge of his erection grow against her and twisted her hips to rub against him. She let her head fall backward so that her hair brushed against his shoulder, and she felt the warm exhalation of his breath against her neck a moment before his lips touched her skin.

She shivered with sensual delight, and it was all she could do not to grab his wrist and lead him to the VIP bathroom.

But she wasn't that woman. Not tonight.

Or was she?

What was wrong with having fun and enjoying a moment like this one? She knew how rarely they came along.

She turned in his arms. His eyes were heavy lidded as he danced and watched her body. She put her hands around his shoulders and moved against him. Their eyes met, and she leaned up to kiss him. His mouth against hers was firm yet also soft at the same time. Better than she remembered.

How was that even possible?

His tongue rubbed against hers as he held her to him with a hand at her hip. They moved together to the music, and she knew she was never going to be able to just walk away from this man.

There was something about him that... *Stop*. She made her mind cancel that thought. This was a hookup—they could both walk away guilt-free and then get back to their real lives.

He lifted his head, breaking the kiss, then put his hands on either side of her face and leaned down, kissing her harder and deeper, sending a pulse of need and desire through her. Her breasts felt heavier, needy, and her center was moist and aching for him. She shifted to rub against his erection, and he broke the kiss again, this time putting his hands on her hips as he maneuvered them both through the crowded dance floor. As soon as they were out of the throng of people, he led her to a quiet hallway and stood in front her, sheltering her body with his as he put one hand on the wall next to her head.

"I want to take you back to my place. No thinking about who we are or anything like that. Just us. One night only."

She almost smiled at the way he was trying to be a good guy. His erection was hard and rigid pressed against her hip. His voice was raspy and raw with need. And he couldn't stop touching her. His finger rubbed up and down the column of her neck. She stood there caught in the sensual web that they were both weaving around each other and knew there was nothing she could do but say yes.

"Where do you live?" she asked.

"Central Park West," he said.

"I'm closer. Let's go to my place," she said.

"Perfect. I have a driver," he said, moving his hand from the wall and reaching into his pocket, which drew her attention to his groin. She caressed him through the front of his pants as he hit a button on his phone and sent the message.

He groaned as she rubbed the tip of his erection, then took her hand in his. "I want to do this when we are alone and I can get you naked."

"Me too," she said. "I need my bag and then I can go."

He led her back to the VIP area and stood by the velvet ropes as she went and grabbed her bag. Siobahn was gone, but there was a note from her friend on her phone that she'd come back if Marielle needed her to.

She texted she was good and didn't mention Inigo. He was her dirty little secret tonight—just as she suspected she was his.

Eight

It took them longer than Inigo anticipated to leave the club, because he couldn't keep his hands off her. There was a sort of haze over him right this moment. All he could see was Marielle. Her lips were wet and swollen from his kisses. *Damn.*

He leaned in to kiss her again. The bouncer held the door for them, and they were caught between the warmth of the club and the snow and sleet falling outside. Inigo pulled her into his body to protect her from the elements. She put her hand on the side of his neck, tipping her head slightly, and he knew she wanted to say something, but her lips were too tempting to resist and he kissed her again.

He wasn't aware of anything but Marielle. He

tucked that fact away to examine later, because he knew that she was the first person to bring on that focus he normally reserved for racing.

"Mr. Velasquez," his driver said, clearing his throat.

He pulled his head from Marielle's and glanced at the driver, noticing he had opened the door. He took her hand and pulled her quickly across the sidewalk through the snow toward the waiting Moretti Motors Vallerio sedan. She slid easily into the back seat, laughing as she sat down and slipped on the leather seats.

He climbed in after her, lifting her off the seat and onto his lap.

She felt chilly from the snow and sleet, and he cuddled her close to him while she ran her fingers through his hair. "You have snowflakes on your eyelashes."

"Do I?"

"You do," she said. "Close your eyes."

He did as she asked and felt the warmth of her breath against his face before she kissed both of his eyes lightly and then settled back onto his lap. "There you go."

He opened his eyes. Their gazes met, and he felt his pulse start racing again. He didn't want to have a quickie in the car. He wanted to make love to her properly. To take his time with Marielle, because maybe if he got her out of his system he could move on. No more rude potshots at her and no more lust that he couldn't control.

He was used to control, and he hated that she made him feel like he had crashed his car and was rolling over and over, like nothing in the world was solid and he was holding on trying to find his center.

With Marielle he was simply holding on to her. And he felt his grip on her was tenuous at best. He should be scared, but instead he was turned on and excited. He couldn't keep his hands off her and she didn't seem to mind, moving to straddle him on the back seat of the car. He held her to him as she deepened the kiss and he clutched at her backside, bring her closer to him as he shifted his hips underneath until he could rub the ridge of his hard-on against her center.

She rocked her hips, moving over him with the kind of pressure that made his pants too tight and made him want to just say screw it and take her here and now.

He moved his hand under the hem of her dress and felt the cold skin of her upper thigh. He rubbed his hand up and down, each time coming closer to touching her center. It was hot and moist and beckoned him. He remembered how hot they had been for each other the last time. If it was even possible, it seemed he wanted her even more now.

He felt the pulse in his erection where it was trapped too tightly in his boxer briefs, and when he pulled his mouth from hers, turning his head hopefully to see something that would distract him, he just met her gaze.

That cool gray gaze of hers was hot, like the heat in the cockpit of his car when he was driving. And the excitement he felt as he approached the finish line, this felt like a victory. He had never thought he'd have her in his arms again. But here she was.

He wanted to make this last. Needed to find his much-lauded self-control.

"What are you thinking?"

"Don't come in the car," he said without thinking.

She threw her head back and laughed. "Damn, speedy. I was thinking, *I hope he comes in the car.*"

"Marielle, darling, you are pushing me to the very edge of my control," he admitted, burying his face in the crook of her neck.

Which was a big old mistake, because she smelled so good. How could perfume be sexy? On her it was.

"Well, then, I'll have to see what I can do to push you past it. I want to see you when you aren't thinking and analyzing everything," she said.

"I'm not sure that's a smart idea," he said.

"I thought we'd decided this wasn't our most intelligent decision," she said, shifting on him to run her finger down the side of his jaw to his mouth. She drew her finger over his lips, and he felt it as if she were caressing his groin.

He groaned and shook his head, sucking her finger into his mouth. He needed to take charge but every time he did, he saw the finish line and he wanted… Marielle and this entire night to last as long as it could.

The car pulled to a stop, and he glanced out the window. They were at his place.

"We forgot to give the driver your address," he said.

"That's okay. We had a nice ride."

The door opened, and a rush of cold air came in, doing nothing to cool him down as he got out and reached back to offer his hand to her. He nodded to the driver, and as Marielle stepped out, Inigo scooped her up in his arms, carrying her toward his building. She wrapped her arms around him, and he lowered his head to kiss her as he stepped into the lobby.

Inigo had never been much of a playboy when it came to women. He liked women and had been on his fair share of dates, but driving was the focus of his life, and no woman had ever held a candle to the rush he got when he was behind the wheel.

His brother had commented that maybe he hadn't met the right woman, and for the first time Inigo understood where Mo had been coming from. Marielle was different; everything with her was more pronounced. When he kissed her, he felt a jolt that was beyond just sexual and maybe…maybe that's why he'd been trying to justify being with her.

Trying to make it into some sort of revenge

scheme so he wouldn't have to admit that she did something to him that no other woman ever had.

Keke and Marco had been circumspect, but Dante hadn't been as nice. He had warned Inigo that it was one thing to get his rocks off with a hot chick but another to have his bosses discussing it. He knew Dante's career was tied to Inigo's winning as well.

Everyone on the team had a vested interest in him winning. So he couldn't let sleeping with her be a distraction.

She wrapped one leg around his thigh as she put her hands in his hair and deepened the kiss. He groaned. He could give himself all the mental warnings he wanted to, but there was no way he was walking away from her tonight.

He couldn't.

He wasn't even tempted to, if he were being completely honest with himself. He carried her down the hall to his apartment and then lifted his head from the kiss, shifting her in his arms and setting her on her feet next to the door.

He used his thumbprint to unlock the door and opened it, stepping aside and gesturing for her to precede him into his place.

She stepped into the foyer of his apartment, and he reached around her to flick on the lights. He closed the door behind them and watched her as she kicked off her heels and slowly walked down the marble-tiled floor toward the living room.

She stood at the base of the curving staircase, her

hand on the mahogany railing, her head tossed back. "I like your place, speedy. Is your bedroom up here?"

His throat felt tight as he closed the distance between them, remembering the feel of her body pressed against his in the club. He wanted her. Maybe more than he wanted to win at Melbourne, which should have jarred him, but for tonight he ignored it. Tomorrow he had to get this attraction for her under control but for tonight…nothing mattered except this feeling and this moment.

She crooked her finger at him, and he groaned as he slowly moved up the stairs toward the landing.

Her thick blond hair fell around her shoulders, and the thin slip dress she wore clung to her curves as she reached behind her and drew the zipper down. He stood beneath her on the stairs watching as she lowered it and her skin was revealed. She had a small tattoo on her left shoulder that he hadn't noticed the first time they'd been together.

He took the steps two at a time to catch up with her. Wrapping his hand around her waist, he pulled her back against him and used his teeth to pull the thin spaghetti strap down her arm. He could see the design of her tattoo more clearly now. It was a serpent wrapped around an apple that had a big bite taken out of it.

He traced it with his finger. "What does this mean to you?"

She shook her head, her long blond hair brushing against the backs of his fingers. "Sinner. Mostly I got it to annoy my mom, but I also knew that I couldn't keep pretending to be something I wasn't."

Sinner. The word echoed in his mind and shook him. Was she as blasé about the affair with Jose as she'd seemed? Or had it cut her deeper?

He stopped thinking about that. He drew his hand down her shoulder blade, her skin was soft and smooth. He felt her shiver under his caress, and she shifted around to face him. As she did so, the dress fell farther down, revealing the curve of her nipped-in waist.

He lifted her off her feet again and carried her down the hall to his bedroom. He hit the light switch with his elbow as he entered and put her on her feet in front of the king-size bed. She smiled up at him.

"What's got your engine roaring?"

He groaned. "Really?"

"I like a good pun," she said with a wink.

"That's not a—"

She let her dress drop to the floor, so she was now standing in front of him wearing just a tiny pair of bikini panties and that smile of hers that would tempt any man to follow her.

He couldn't think. He reached for her breasts. He was rock-hard and on fire for her. Each breath he took smelled of her perfume, and his heartbeat seemed to be saying her name. *Marielle. Marielle. Marielle.*

He put one hand on her waist to draw her to him, but she wedged her hand between them, her fingers going to the buttons of his shirt, slowly undoing them. He watched her for a minute then realized he had a nearly naked woman in his arms.

She touched him in a way that made him feel like the only man in the world. Her eyes were heavy lidded as she leaned forward, kissing his neck as she drew her nails down the center of his body. Blood rushed through his veins, pooling in his groin and making him even harder as she caressed her way down his body.

Her fingers were cool against his skin as she pushed the shirt off his torso. He shrugged out of it and drew her into his arms, enjoying the feel of her naked breasts against him.

A growl was torn from him when her hot mouth brushed over the column of his throat. She took her time nibbling her way down his neck to his chest, biting his left pec, which made him jump in surprise. She looked up at him, her gray eyes sparkling. "Too much?"

"Not enough," he said, his eyes narrowing as he reached down to undo the fastening of his pants and give his erection more room. Her tongue brushed his nipple, and gooseflesh spread over his chest and back. His hips jerked forward, and she reached out, pushing her hand into the opening of his pants, rubbing her palm over him.

He ran his hands over the length of her naked back. He wanted to believe that his excitement was just because it had been so long since he'd been with a woman, but he knew that this was more about Marielle. She was forbidden fruit. His boss had mentioned her by name, his sister hated her and his best friend thought she was trouble.

But he couldn't resist. He'd always been the sensible Velasquez, but had that all been an illusion? Was it simply because he'd been going too fast to realize that he was just as impulsive as his brothers?

Marielle wasn't shy when it came to touching him, and he loved it. Bracing herself with her hands on his shoulders, she slowly traced each of his ribs before moving lower.

Part of him wanted to let her do whatever she wanted, but another part of him was aware that this was only the second time in a year that he'd had sex, and he was on edge. His control wasn't as great as it once had been. She rubbed her fingertip along his belt, tracing it around his waist and then coming back to the lowered zipper. He sucked in his breath and held it until she winked at him.

She took the shaft of his erection in her hand, stroking him through his underwear. He felt his erection jump and a bit of moisture form on the tip. He wasn't going to make it much longer. He tugged her into his arms, holding her so that her bare breasts brushed against his chest.

Leaning back on the bed, he used his hands to part her thighs and drew her down on his lap. He pushed his underwear down to free his length and then shifted his hips until he felt her warmth against his tip.

He knew he should get a condom on, but for this moment he wanted to savor the feeling of her heat against his naked shaft. He stretched to reach the nightstand and took out a condom, handing it to her.

Then he lifted her up with his arm around her waist and tugged her panties off her body. She settled back on his thighs, tearing open the condom and putting it on him.

She straddled him and he put his hands on her waist, drawing her down. He tried to let her set the pace, but she was in the mood to tease him and he was already on the knife's edge. He cupped her buttocks and drew her down hard as he thrust up inside her. Driving himself all the way into her body, he held himself there.

She gripped his shoulders with her hands, her nails digging into his skin as their mouths met. Her nipples were hard points and he pulled away from her mouth, glancing down to see them pushing against his chest.

He caressed her back and spine, scraping his nails down the length of it. He followed the line of her back down to the indentation above her backside.

She closed her eyes and held her breath as he fondled her, running his finger over her nipple. It was velvety compared to the satin smoothness of her breast. He brushed his finger back and forth until she bit her lower lip and shifted on his lap.

She moaned a sweet sound that he leaned up to capture in her mouth. She tipped her head to the side, immediately allowing him access to her mouth. She stayed like that, straddling him so that just the tip of his erection was inside her.

He scraped his fingernail over her nipple, and she shivered in his arms. He pushed her back a little bit so he could see her. Her breasts were bare, nipples distended and begging for his mouth. He lowered his head and suckled.

He held her still with a hand on the small of her back. He buried his other hand in her hair and arched her over his arm. Both of her breasts were thrust up at him.

He wouldn't let this be about anything other than the physical. One night for revenge, he'd thought, but this was the second time they'd been together. And revenge wasn't on his mind.

She rocked her hips, trying to take him deeper, and he knew the time for teasing was at an end.

He gave her another inch, thrusting up into her sweet, tight body. Her eyes were closed, her hips moving subtly against him, and when he blew on her nipple, he saw gooseflesh spread down her body.

He loved the way she reacted to his mouth on her. He sucked on the skin at the base of her neck as he thrust all the way home, sheathing his entire length in her body. He knew he was leaving a mark with his mouth, and that pleased him. He wanted her to remember this moment and what they had done when she was alone later.

He kept kissing and rubbing, pinching her nipples until her hands clenched in his hair and she rocked her hips harder against his length. He lifted his hips, thrusting up against her.

Her eyes widened with each inch he gave her. She clutched at his hips as he started thrusting. She held him to her, eyes half-closed and her head tipped back.

He leaned down and caught one of her nipples in his teeth, scraping very gently. She started to tighten around him. Her hips moved faster, demanding more, but he kept the pace slow, steady. Building the pleasure between them.

He suckled her nipple and rotated his hips to catch her pleasure point with each thrust. He felt her hands clenching in his hair as she threw her head back.

He varied his thrusts, finding a rhythm that would draw out the tension at the base of his spine. Something that would make his time in her body, wrapped in her silky limbs, last forever.

He tensed, blood roaring in his ears, as he felt everything in his world center on this one woman.

He called her name as he came. She tightened around him and he looked down into her eyes as he kept thrusting. He saw her eyes widen and felt the minute contractions of her body around his as she was consumed by her orgasm.

He rotated his hips until her hips stopped rocking

against him. She wrapped her arms around his shoulders and kissed the underside of his chin.

He wanted to believe that nothing had changed, but he knew that everything had. Revenge had seemed like the only solution until now. He was starting to care for Marielle, seeing beyond the woman who'd hurt his sister to the woman who was vulnerable and sexy—and everything he hadn't realized he'd been looking for.

Nine

Not sure if she'd stayed or left, he was almost reluctant to get out of bed. But he had never been the sort of man who hid from anything, so he did. He used the bathroom and then heard piano music downstairs. The living room of his apartment had a baby grand piano because Bianca had said it would photograph well when *Urban Living* magazine did a spread on him. He pulled on his Moretti Motors sweatpants and a T-shirt and went downstairs more quickly than he normally did, skipping his set of morning reps.

There she was, standing over the piano, her fingers nimbly picking out the melody of a classical piece that he struggled to identify. He was pretty sure it was Debussy, but his musical leanings were more toward rap.

"Morning," he said.

She turned and smiled at him, backlit by the lights in the hallway that led to the kitchen. Her long silvery-blond hair was loose and hung over her shoulders. She wore one of his shirts, her long legs bare. His gut clenched. He'd meant for last night to be the last time they were together. Both of them were on the same page as far as that was concerned. But this morning there was none of the awkwardness that had dominated their other morning after.

The music stopped, and she glanced over at him. Her eyes were sleepy, but she flashed him a smile. "I hope I didn't wake you."

"You didn't," he admitted. "I have a testing session I need to get to. I wasn't sure you'd still be here."

"I was going to leave but didn't want to slink out. We didn't say goodbye last time. And this time... well, I thought we needed that. To make sure it's officially ended," she said.

"Definitely," he agreed. "Do you need some clothes?"

"My assistant is bringing some stuff over for me," she said. "I don't think I'd look as good in your sweats as you do."

He smiled at the way she said it. She was keeping things light, and he would do the same. "Bianca keeps some clothes here."

"I don't want to wear your sister's clothes."

"Of course not." Clearly, he needed coffee. That had been…the wrong thing to say.

"Coffee?" he asked her.

"Do you have green tea?"

"I think I might have some. I'll go and check," he said, moving farther into the living room, walking past her into the kitchen. As soon as he was in the kitchen, he let out a breath he hadn't realized he was holding.

He still wanted her.

How was that possible?

Last night should have cured him of the desire for her. But to be fair, what guy could resist Marielle wearing his T-shirt and playing the piano? It was so sexy and sensual, and it literally took everything in him to keep from walking back in there and seducing her on the piano bench.

He went to the big espresso machine he'd been gifted last year when he'd done an ad for the company and flicked on the button to start the warm-up process. Then he realized he had no idea where his housekeeper might store tea.

He started opening up cabinets and then stopped. She wasn't playing anymore, and he knew his comment about Bianca had affected her. He didn't need to do anything more than get her some tea—if he could f-ing find it—and then go to training.

He finally found the cupboard stash of tea. It was a mahogany case he'd been given when he'd done the fastest qualifying lap at the Singapore Grand Prix last year.

He walked back to the living room, where she was sitting at the piano but looking at her phone. Her shoulders were slumped, and to him it seemed like she'd gotten bad news.

"You okay?" he asked.

"Yup. Jim dandy," she said. "My dad always says that. No idea what it really means."

"My dad says things that I really don't get too," Inigo said, coming over to her. "I found this. Any tea in here excite you?"

She took the case from him and set it on the bench beside her, finally opening it up and looking through the selection. She handed him a tea bag, and he took it, along with the case. "When did you learn to play the piano?"

"Starting when I was six. One of my brothers showed an aptitude, and my parents thought I might enjoy it too. I think they thought we'd be this famous classical duo for a while. But Leo lost interest when he hit puberty. Apparently, girls were more interesting than piano."

Inigo smiled. "And you stopped?"

"I was the add-on child, so it seemed best," she said.

"Add-on?"

"Sorry. I'm dealing with some family stuff and feeling like a total bitch about them," she admitted.

"I'm sorry too. Want to talk about it? Or should I just go and get your tea?"

She looked over at him. "Why do you have to be a Velasquez?"

He sat down next to her, putting his arm around her shoulder and hugging her close for a minute. "I don't know," he said, then after a moment of silence, continued. "Tell me about this thing with your family," he said. "It will make us both stop thinking about each other."

"I don't think it's going to work that easily."

He used his knuckles on the black keys to play the one thing he could, the riff on "The Knuckle Song." And she smiled, as he hoped she would. "We won't know if we don't try."

"Fair enough," she said. "My dad had an affair two years before I was born. He was a prominent congressman, and the identity of the young aide he'd had the affair with was found out—it was a big scandal everywhere. My dad realized he could be 'that cliché mid-life crisis guy.' That's how he puts it. Like that explains everything. Darian, my oldest brother, said that it changed Mom. I've always been her consolation baby. I showed how my parents got back together and proved to the world that they were still solid."

She shouldn't have brought up the circumstances of her birth. Not to Inigo. But she was feeling down, and in this sort of mood she got destructive. And it wasn't like he was thinking of her as anything other than his booty call from last night. Even if they wanted it to be more, there was no way. He'd confirmed that when he'd sat down next to her on the piano bench.

Playing the piano had started her down this path—or maybe it was waking up next to him. She would deny it out loud, but she'd slept better in his arms than she had in a long time.

"That's horrible. I'm sure that's not true," he said. "When you were a kid, it might have seemed that way to you, but your parents love you."

She started laughing. "How would you even guess at that? Do you think you know them from articles and TV documentaries?"

"No. I'm just basing it on my own parents. When I was a kid, I thought that they liked my twin brothers best because they always got the most attention. It was only as I aged that I realized they needed the most attention. The rest of us were pretty self-sufficient. Diego has always been more at home with horses than people. Bianca was into fashion and her own thing, and I had racing."

Marielle looked over at him. He was an odd contradiction—at times brutally honest and then sweet. She wished she were wrong about her parents but she knew she wasn't, given that her mom was still very reluctant to even invite her to events she was in charge of. The thing was, 85 percent of the time Marielle didn't care about what her parents thought.

She was busy doing her own thing, and so were they. It was just when she needed something…did they ever come through for her without giving her a hard time? If she could just say screw it to her mom and not attend the events, it would be much easier.

"That's nice, but I really am a reminder that he cheated and she wanted to leave. But he talked her into staying. I was supposed to make things better between them…but my mom had a difficult pregnancy and birth. She also didn't like having a daughter as much as she thought, and everyone was surprised that my dad took an interest in me. He hadn't really spent a lot of time with the boys when they were babies…anyhow, that just made it worse with the two of them. And they did a shit ton of press after my birth because Carlton—he's Dad's head of staff—thought it would help in the polls."

Inigo just stared at her, and she realized that she'd laid too much truth out there. But she got tired of lugging it around, and this morning her guard was down.

He didn't say anything. He just pulled her into his arms and hugged her closely to him. "God, what a mess."

She smiled.

He'd said just the right thing. Again.

Why couldn't she have met him instead of Jose all those years ago?

But she hadn't.

"It really is. You already know the worst side of me, so sharing it with you doesn't seem so bad."

"I'm glad. Despite everything else, I'm glad we had this night together."

She nodded and looked away from him, back at the keyboard. "Yeah, me too."

"Why were you thinking of them?"

She shook her head. She wasn't going there. Not with Inigo and not this morning. They were essentially strangers with the hots for each other, and that was good enough. She decided she'd done enough soul baring for now.

"Who knows," she said. "So…what exactly does a testing session entail?"

"I'm trying out different cockpit setups at the facility. My engineering team has made some adjustments from my last run in the simulator. We load up the different tracks and then the weather conditions and my placement to see how I react to different variables."

She shifted on the bench, tucking one leg underneath her as she studied him. "That's fascinating. When I worked for F1, I really never knew much of what the drivers did when they weren't at the track."

"Yeah, there's a hell of a lot more involved than just getting behind the wheel. Some of the technical stuff fascinates me, and because I'm good friends with one of the engineers I know more about that part than some drivers. But most of it is over my head. I mean, I tell them what I want the car to do, and they make tweaks either here at the facility or in the trailer at the track and the car is adjusted. It's cool."

She smiled. He was so cute when he was getting all nerdy about cars. Mentally she slapped herself. She couldn't fall for him. They could never be friends. There was too much heat and too much baggage between the two of them for that to ever happen.

"So, you want your tea?" he asked after a few minutes.

"Yes," she said as her phone pinged with a message. "My assistant is downstairs with my clothes."

"Great. I'll let the doorman know to let her up."

"Him. It's PJ."

"Okay," Inigo said and hit a button on his smartphone to let the doorman know that her assistant was okay to come up. He slid off the bench and stood there for a minute.

"I liked your piano playing. No matter why you learned, it's part of you, and you shouldn't deny it."

Then he left to go back into the kitchen, and she could only watch him leave. And firmly remind herself this time their goodbye was for good.

Inigo wasn't surprised when he got to the Moretti Motors testing facility to see that Dante was already behind his computer working away. Matteo was running a circuit on the Melbourne track, and both of the bosses were observing from their conference room. He'd heard that Malcolm had been invited out to the track so that when he went to place his bet those running the betting ring would think he had inside information.

Inigo rubbed the back of his neck. The dancing and the sex with Marielle had completely zoned him out. He was so chill right now that he wasn't sure if he was going to be good behind the wheel or not. Normally he was tense and focused. But this chill feeling wasn't that bad.

"Inigo, hop in the cockpit and let's see if this setup is working for you."

He walked over and started the process of buckling himself in. He put on his helmet and then flexed his fingers, cracking his knuckles and gripping the steering wheel. He heard everything his engineers were saying as they cued him up. Then he waited for the green light and took off on the simulated track. His instincts were more heightened then they had been the last time. The car seemed an extension of him, and he moved through each turn and curve with ease. He kept accelerating, and he knew he was having the drive of his life. He didn't question it—he just did the laps. When he stopped, there was silence on the headset.

"Guys? How was it?"

"Good...damn good. We need to check a few things," Dante said.

Inigo got out of the simulator and noticed that everyone was working at their monitors. Had his chill attitude made him drive like a rookie? Had that drive of his life really been a huge mistake?

"How'd it go last night?" Dante asked when Inigo walked over to him.

"Good, man, the best," he said. "What's up with my time?"

"We are still checking a few things. I've sent my data over—we should hear something in a minute," Dante said, spinning around to face him. "So last night was good…guess you gave up the revenge thing?"

"Yeah," he said. "I mean, it's not like I'll see her again. Last night…was goodbye."

Dante just chuckled and shook his head. "If anyone else said that to me, I'd call them a liar, but I know you have ice in your veins when it comes to women."

"I'm not cold," Inigo said.

"Dude, you are. And that was envy you heard. I wish I could be more like you," Dante said. "Relationships are messy, but you always skate right by them. And it's not like the women you hook up with hate you later. They're cool too."

Inigo wasn't sure he liked the way Dante was describing him. He couldn't argue with his friend because his description was spot-on, but he didn't know if that was the kind of man he wanted to be.

"Yeah, lucky me," he said, feeling some tension seeping into his Zen attitude.

Marco came into the room with Keke behind him. Both men had a look on their faces that Inigo hadn't seen before. He felt nervous. Hell, why had he slept with Marielle last night? His celibacy during the racing season had sort of been his way of making sure he stayed in the right headspace to race. Of course, last night he hadn't been thinking about the season or his time.

It had all been Marielle.

Which had felt so damned good at the time, but now, in retrospect, he regretted it. Maybe it was because he knew she was forbidden fruit, or maybe it was just that he didn't like to have anyone walk away from him. He was always the one who left, he thought, but with Marielle it had been different.

"Inigo, we want you to drive again. Your time was faster than Matteo's and the best you've ever done," Marco said, his Italian accent slightly more pronounced than usual.

"Whatever you did last time," Keke said, clapping him on the shoulder, "do it again."

"Yeah, okay. I can do that," he said. But now he was worried he couldn't, and he knew that was going to mess with his mind. He stepped away from everyone, turned his back on the room and remembered the way Marielle had been when he'd left her this morning. She'd still been sitting at the piano playing some classical song as she'd watched him leave.

Leaving had been hard; he'd wanted to go back and make love to her right there on the piano bench. He felt that chill feeling sweep over him again. He was getting back to that numb mind space where he was able to feel physically sated from the night before but with that tiny tinge of excitement that he could have her again tonight.

He didn't bother to let doubt or anything other than that calm but edgy feeling fill him as he turned and walked over to the cockpit of the simulator. Everyone stepped back and let him do his thing. Even the engineers who helped strap him in didn't speak to him. They were used to drivers and their rituals. Inigo flexed his fingers and cracked his knuckles as he always did and then put his hands on the wheel.

There was no room in his mind for doubt, and as they counted down to starting, he let go of everything that didn't serve the course. He became one with the car the way he always did, felt the road underneath the wheels even though it was just a simulation. As he maneuvered around the track with ease, the car responded to him the way Marielle had last night. Every touch was strategically placed to keep the car purring and doing exactly what he wanted it to do.

When he stopped and got out of the simulator, he looked over at Marco and Keke, who were standing at Dante's station. Both men let out a whoop, and Inigo knew he'd done it again.

But it wasn't just him…it had been Marielle. The woman he'd mentally and of course literally said goodbye to looked as if she were the key to him driving and posting the fastest time of his career.

Well, hell.

Ten

Malcolm left the Moretti Motors facility and drove back into the city after texting the bookie he'd been dealing with for the racing bets. He then pulled off on the side of the highway and texted his best friend, Mauricio Velasquez. Mo called back instead of texting.

"Hey, what's up? You said you were going to be in New York for a few more days?" Mo asked.

"Yes. The Moretti thing is really blowing up. I thought if you had any clients you wanted me to meet with while I was here, that might be a good thing. I need to keep my focus and remember that gambling isn't paying my bills, my job is."

"Got it. I'll send you some information. Actually,

there's a property I'm trying to get that's in Hadley's old building. One of her neighbors owns it. I think Helena met her once, and of course she knows all about me, so she doesn't want me to be her agent even though I'm licensed to sell in New York—but she's ticked at what I put Hadley through, but she'd probably talk to you. Got time to do that today?" Mo asked.

Mo and Hadley had been through a lot. At a certain point, Mo had hooked up with someone else while still texting Hadley he wanted her back. She'd come back to town to surprise him and found another woman in his bed. She'd broken up with him on the spot and moved to New York before Mo had realized he was an idiot to let her slip away and set about winning her back once Hadley had moved back to Cole's Hill.

"Yes," Malcolm said. "I definitely do. I don't want to be lingering with the bookie looking at the racing form and thinking I could use the money to get rich quick."

"Good. You doing okay?" Mo asked. "Inigo can find someone else if you're not sure you can handle it. It hasn't been that long since you stopped."

Was he doing okay?

No.

Hell, no.

But his fiancée and her family had asked him to use his expertise—which was also his weakness— to help them, and he wasn't going to let them down.

Nothing had compared to how he'd felt when he had let Helena down the first time. He'd promised himself he'd never do it again.

And this was nothing. Just a little walk through fire, but hey, he could handle this. He needed to prove to himself that he was stronger now. That he wouldn't fall again. Because Helena wanted the whole enchilada with him. Kids, golden anniversary, growing old together. He couldn't fall back into his old habit. He needed this.

To prove to her and to himself that he had really conquered this.

"Yeah, I'm good. I just needed to talk. Sometimes it's good to get out of my head," Mal said.

"I know what you mean. Talking to you and to Hadley is what keeps me from giving in to my anger…but honestly, I'm mellower now than I've ever been in my life. My dad thinks it's because of Hadley. He said getting laid regularly does that."

Malcolm laughed. "Your dad is too much."

"He really is. I hope I'm still having fun when I'm old like him."

"Goals right there."

They both laughed, and then Mo asked, "Seriously, you okay?"

"Yeah. I am. With Helena here, and talking to you, it keeps me clear. Helps me stay in the real world, not that gambler's red haze where it seems like one bet could make me a tycoon."

"A tycoon? Seriously?" Mauricio asked.

"Yeah. Like the Monopoly dude," Malcolm said, feeling much more normal now. "That's why I got into real estate."

"You know what? Me too. I mean, it helped getting that house in town to fix up the summer between my freshman and sophomore year in college, but once I started flipping houses, I realized how much money could be made with a good eye."

"You definitely have the eye," Malcolm said. He did appreciate all that Mo had taught him about real estate. He had been floundering at the agency he'd worked at before Mo had brought him on board. He never could forget what his friend had done for him.

He'd given him focus and a chance to become the man he wanted to be. A man Helena could be proud to call her own.

"You do too. I'm glad to have you on my team," Mo said. "I'll send that info over. Let me know if you need anything else."

They hung up, and Malcolm got back on the road. It was good to know that this favor for Moretti Motors wasn't the only thing on his plate today. He needed his real job and real life around him.

Helena was waiting for him in the lobby when he got back from Moretti Motors, and she rushed over to him as soon as she saw him, hugging him and then stepping back to look up into his face.

"How'd it go?"

"Great. Straightforward and easy," he said. "Do you feel up to coming with me to meet a real estate client? It's an apartment in Hadley's old building. I thought afterward you could show me that bagel place you and Hadley always rave about."

She nodded. "Yes. I'd love to. Are we staying in New York for a while?"

"No. One more night and then we're heading home. But this is a client who probably won't deal with Mo because she knew about the drama between him and Hadley."

"Ah. His womanizing ways catching up to him."

"Something like that," Malcolm said. It felt good to have Helena by his side. He was worried when he saw how concerned she'd been. But seeing the way she kept giving him glances when she thought he wasn't looking just drove home the point that she still wasn't sure of him.

He felt that tension start in the back of his neck. Sometimes it was really hard not to feel as if Helena and her entire family were judging him. He knew he came from the poorer side of town. And Mr. Everton had made it clear that marrying his daughter wasn't a shortcut to the country club set. Which was fine, since that was something Malcolm had never aspired to. He just wanted to live with the woman he loved.

She slipped her hand in his.

"I don't know if I could do what you're doing," she said, going up on tiptoe and kissing him. "You have way more courage than I do."

Her words were a balm for his soul, and he let them soothe the tension away.

* * *

Marielle had texted Darian and told him never mind, she'd handle her mom and Carlton without him. He'd only responded that he was there if she needed him, but she was pretty sure she wouldn't. After she'd spilled her guts to Inigo, she'd realized how much of that childhood resentment she'd been using to feed her journey as an adult. She'd been making choices for a long time just to annoy her mom.

It was like she was still jumping in the pool yelling, *hey, Mom, watch me*, to a woman who would rather sip her martini and gossip with her friends. She'd had such a feeling of clarity when she'd left Inigo's place that it had been almost like a weight was lifted from her.

It would be nice to use her family connections, but she didn't need them. She'd been very content with building her influencer career based on doing the things she loved. The things that suited her. It would be a huge shortcut to have her mom invite her to her top-tier events, but at the same time, it wasn't the end of the world if she didn't.

When she got back to her apartment, she had to prepare and write a series of posts. Her photographer was coming over just after lunch to do a photo shoot for a sponsored post that she'd be running next week. The sponsor was the luxury jewelry brand House of Hamilton. They were trying to promote their name to a younger crowd and, in the words of the PR manager, home in on the blue box market.

Her phone pinged, and she saw it was a message in her Snapchat group from Siobahn.

Did you hit it last night?

Yes. It was good. Not like it could have been.

I'm in the studio until six. Can you hang out?

Maybe. I have a call in to my mom. I need to go and see her. You down for a drive to the Hamptons?

No. But when you're back ping me.

She set her phone aside and went to fill up her water bottle, and when she came back, she saw that Siobahn had sent another message that said if she needed her, she'd go with her.

She smiled to herself. She'd always felt so isolated by her feelings of inadequacy, which in retrospect had made her easy pickings for a man like Jose. She felt like she didn't deserve a man who was free to be hers, so that was what she'd attracted. And it would be easy to place the blame on her mom, but the truth was whenever she'd been presented with two choices, she always leaned toward the one that would cause the most grief for her parents.

Her phone rang, and she saw it was her parents'

house phone in the Hamptons. She took a deep breath before she answered the call. She felt the tension in her shoulders, and that knot in the pit of her stomach appeared as it always did when she thought of speaking to her parents...or worse, Carlton.

"This is Marielle," she said, using the manners and etiquette that her mother had drilled into her as a child. She always introduced herself. Her mother thought it was the height of arrogance for someone to assume they knew who you were.

"Hello," her mom said. "I'm afraid we have a dinner party scheduled for tonight, but I'm coming to the city for a luncheon and could meet you for coffee at Ralph's after. Let's say three o'clock. Would that work for you?"

Her mom's tone was quiet, as if she wasn't too sure of what Marielle's reaction would be. It was one of the few times she could remember her mother suggesting the two of them do something together and alone. "Yes, I can do that."

"Great. I'll add you to my calendar. See you then," her mom said, ending the call.

Marielle set the phone down and thought about her mom. She didn't really seem like she wanted to change, and Marielle knew she had to be careful not to project onto her mother the feelings of the relationship she wanted. Her therapist had helped her realize that.

Ugh.

Why did life have to be so complicated?

The doorbell rang, and she heard PJ answer it. A moment later he came in with a vase of pink peonies. "For you."

"Wow. Very nice. I wonder who they're from?" she asked. Maybe the brand she'd met with the other day.

She pulled out the card once PJ went back to his tablet to answer some DMs she had received. He screened most of them and provided answers she'd already written to her most commonly asked questions.

She opened the card and saw the printed message.

Thanks for last night. Would you have dinner with me tonight? I'd like to discuss possibly seeing each other again.
Inigo

She read it, then reread it.

What the hell?

They'd already discovered they were oil and water—they didn't match. It didn't matter that they went up like flames when they were together. This dance they were playing with each other had to end.

Yet she didn't want to say no.

She sort of did want to see him again. He had made her see her world in a way that she'd never looked at it before, and though a part of her felt like she was using him, another part was eager to see what would be revealed if she spent more time with him.

Dinner at his place sent a certain message. Exactly the one he wanted her to receive—that he was happy to hook up, but that was it.

He shoved his hand through his hair.

This had stupid written all over it.

But he needed to see if sleeping with Marielle was making him faster. Marco had seen a picture of him and Marielle from the night before when they'd been getting into the car. Apparently, the paparazzi had been watching the door. He couldn't remember anything but wanting to be alone with her.

Marco had said that he'd had a woman change his driving: his wife. Which made Inigo reluctant to continue anything with Marielle. He hadn't said anything to his boss about the fact that she had been Jose's mistress. But Dante had looked up his times later, and they'd notice a slight uptick.

Now that he thought about it, it made him feel sort of sick. Was he really using her because he thought she'd made him faster?

The simple answer was yes. The championship had eluded him for too long. But he also knew that he couldn't just use her. He had to be clear about his intentions.

God, he felt like his dad. Was it an old-fashioned sentiment? She wasn't looking for a ring from him.

She had her own thing going. She didn't need him, did she? Sex was just that—sex.

Why did he feel a knot in his stomach at the thought of that?

She'd been different from the beginning. He couldn't say it was just because he'd ended his self-imposed celibacy. It was more than that.

This was something else. Once again he felt that tension at the back of his neck that warned him this might not be as straightforward as he wanted it to be.

But he wasn't willing to let go of her if it meant winning.

He'd sent flowers, and she'd agreed to come to dinner. He had ordered from one of his favorite restaurants, and they had sent over a sous chef to prepare and serve the food in his dining room that overlooked Central Park. The city was blanketed in snow from a cold snap, and as he looked out the window, he almost had to pinch himself.

Driving had given him this life. It wasn't like he had grown up struggling. He'd had nice things; his father was a horse rancher and he'd grown up in a world of wealth and privilege. But this was different. He'd earned this. This was his.

His phone vibrated with a message from the doorman that Marielle was here. He texted to send her up and then alerted the chef that they would be ready to eat in thirty minutes or so.

He went to the door to wait for her. She arrived a few minutes later, her hair pulled into a loose ponytail low at the back of her neck. It wasn't one of those messy buns that so many women wore these days. She had on a pair of skinny leather leggings and a soft-looking sweater that hugged the curves of her breasts and made it damned near impossible for him to look away. But he finally did.

He smiled when she waggled both of her eyebrows at him.

"I thought we'd decided last night was goodbye," she said, walking into his apartment.

"Plans change," he said. He was thrown into doubt about whether to tell her that she'd made him faster.

He was a mess right now. What if it wasn't her? He'd been really focused over the last year.

Dante had warned him that he was going to have to be careful about attributing too much to Marielle.

"They do. So…"

"I have a private chef making dinner for us, but can I get you a drink?" he asked.

"Are you drinking?" she asked. "I thought you were sticking to ice water during the racing season."

"I am. Well, pretty much all the time. Plus, my brother Mauricio has a short tempter, and I found when I drink, I do too. And I saw how destructive that was for him…so I avoid it whenever I can."

"Fair enough," she said. "I'm fine with soda water and a twist of lime."

"Coming right up. If you want to have a seat by the fire, I'll bring the drinks," he said.

He'd lit a fire in the fireplace, thinking it would

be more romantic than sitting on the couch with *SportsCenter* playing in the background. But maybe that would have sent a different message. He realized he was standing at the bar looking down at the limes that the chef had prepared earlier and wondering how he'd ever thought he could get revenge on her. He couldn't even find a way to tell her about how she'd affected him at the test today.

He felt like some kind smarmy dude even thinking about how he would suggest that they hook up so his times could keep getting faster.

"Inigo?"

Startled, he spilled some of the soda water he'd just poured as he turned to her.

"What's going on?" she asked. "I've never seen you move this slow before or be so jumpy. You're usually moving faster than the speed of light and smooth as hell."

He handed her the drink after he wiped the glass down with a napkin. "I have a proposition for you."

"Ooh. I'm intrigued. Is it an indecent proposal?"

He felt his face flush. She threw her head back and laughed. "Okay, let's hear it. Though I have to be honest and tell you that if you offer me less than a cool million, I'm going to be insulted."

She always surprised him, never reacting the way he expected. "Money would sully what we have."

He felt like he was getting some of his mojo back. She made him feel calm…well, horny as hell, but calm inside. And he had to wonder if that was all he needed from her. But why would he turn down sex if she agreed?

Eleven

Once again he had surprised her, but really, should she have been? They were both dancing around the attraction between them, neither of them wanting to admit that there could be anything more than sex.

But could there be?

"So…no money," she joked. But what did he want? She wondered sometimes why she never found a normal guy who just wanted to chat on a dating app and then meet for a meal. Instead she had this… something she wasn't sure she actually minded.

"I feel like it might be better to talk about over dinner. I had a plan," he said.

"But that's not going to work," she said. "You can't bring something like this up and then let it go.

That's not how this works. You said you had a proposition for me."

She'd been told she was too blunt. Her aunt Tilly had warned her more than once to slow down and let her tongue catch up with her mind. It never hurt to give something a thought or two before she blurted it out. But that didn't really suit her. It never had.

"Um, so, today at practice I clocked the fastest time I've ever had. We did it three times to see if it was a fluke. There was a new setup, but that isn't enough to get the kind of speed I got out of the simulator today. It was everything coming together for me. And I think that was because of last night," he said, turning away from her to look out the window.

She lived on the other side of the park, and their views were different. She moved over to stand next to him.

He had just articulated what she'd felt today. Sex had been sort of a detox of all the junk that had been plaguing her lately, and she wouldn't mind trying it again. But she knew from the past when she had tried to justify a relationship—the one with Jose—it hadn't really worked. She feared what she had with Inigo would quickly become something different than what had happened last night, especially since there was still bad blood with his sister.

"I had a moment of clarity today too. I think it was talking to you that made it possible."

"I want to do more than talk," he said sardonically.

"I figured," she said. "But that helped me. You

gave me some perspective that I hadn't been able to find before this."

"So we can hook up for me and talk for you," he said, then shook his head. "That sounds even crazier out loud than it does in my head."

She had to agree it did sound crazy. "I can't go on the Formula One tour with you."

She wasn't going back there again. All of those cities were tied to memories of Jose and now tinged with the fact that he'd been playing her the entire time. She didn't want to have to deal with that. Not now that she was sort of getting herself back on track.

Inigo rubbed the back of his neck, turned to put his drink on the bar and then walked back over to her. "I don't even know if you're what is making a difference in my driving."

"So?"

He shook his head. "I don't know. I had a vague idea of what I was going to suggest, but being here with you, there's no way I can do it. There's something douchy about saying to a woman, *hey, let's hook up so I can see if sex is making me better at my job.*"

She couldn't help the smile that broke across her face. She shook her head. This. This was exactly why she was here in his apartment, despite the fact that he had said some truly mean things to her in the past and would probably do so again. He was unpredictable and at the same time so honest...which was why she knew he'd say something to her again that would hurt. He didn't have that bullshit filter that most of the men she dated in the past had. The one that allowed them to say things to her that she'd believe even though they were lying.

"No, you can't say that. But I'd be willing to try it again," she said. "I like you, Inigo. We can't ever have a relationship, because as much as I don't like Bianca, she's your sister. But the sex is good, you're funny and I enjoy being around you."

He tipped his head to the side, studying her for a few minutes. It felt longer than waiting in the line at Ralph's during rush hour. She had no idea what he was hoping to find in her expression, so she tried to look neutral and then started to feel self-conscious. She ended up just turning to stare out the window. Snow was falling, and from up here it looked peaceful. Like being inside a snow globe.

From up here she could have one of those picture-perfect lives—the one that her followers on social media thought she had. She reached for her phone. But the reflection off the plate glass didn't make a good photo.

"What are you doing?"

"Waiting for you and trying to figure out if I can capture the pristine snow falling on the city. From up here it seems…"

"Ideal."

She nodded. Ideal. That was a good word.

"So are we doing this?" she asked.

"Let's have dinner and then decide," he said. "When you mentioned Bianca, it made me realize that I hadn't thought of how this would affect anyone but you and me."

"We are the only ones who have a stake in this," she said. Was his sister really going to be mad that he was dating her? Probably. Marielle would be ticked off if one of her brothers had dated a girl that had cheated with her ex. She sighed.

"Okay."

Dinner was good, but honestly, Inigo wasn't in a frame of mind to savor it. He wished he'd stuck to his plan, but instead he had sat awkwardly across from Marielle thinking about the dumb-ass way he'd propositioned her. He'd meant to be smoother about it. To be Mr. Charming for once in his life. He should have called Diego. His older brother was good at knowing the right thing to say.

But he didn't really want to let his family know that he'd been sleeping with the woman Bianca hated. Over and over as they ate the meal, that was all he could think of. Marielle was working hard, trying to keep the conversation going, but he knew he was giving her nothing. Just one-word answers and long drawn-out silences between topics.

He'd never been this awkward with a woman.

His phone vibrated in his pocket, and he took it out to see that Keke was downstairs and wanted to come up.

"Uh, one of my bosses is here," he said to Marielle.

"Okay," she said. "Do you want me to leave?"

"No. I've been so horrible, I need a chance to make it up to you. Let me see what he wants," Inigo said.

He texted that it was okay for him to come up. "At least we will have someone to help make conversation."

"Yeah. I had no idea that I would ever work this hard to talk about nothing," she said.

"I'm sorry. It's not like me to say something inappropriate to a woman and then totally shut down," he said.

"I know. I get it. We really shouldn't be doing this. It doesn't matter if you think I'm the reason you drove faster today. Given our connection through Jose, we can't ever do this," she said.

"I know. I had forgotten," he said. "I mean, not really. But when I see you, Marielle, I don't think about Jose or the past. But it is there."

Before she could answer, he heard Keke's hard knock on the door and went to answer it. The German stood there with a big grin on his face, filling the doorway. Next to him was his wife, Elena.

"Sorry to stop by unannounced, but I had an idea that I wanted you to think about tonight," Keke said, coming in. He glanced over at the table and saw Marielle then looked back at Inigo.

"You have a date?"

"Yes, I do," he said.

KATHERINE GARBERA   149

"See, I told you to call first," Elena said. "Nothing can sway him when he starts thinking about racing," she added to Inigo.

She brushed past Keke and walked over to Marielle. She introduced herself and then suggested that they take a bottle of wine and get comfy. "It's supposed to be date night. Our first in three months, but Keke...well, racing is his first love."

"Woman, you know I love you more than racing. But Inigo and I need to discuss this. I promise we won't be more than thirty minutes."

"I've heard that before," Elena said, then looped her arm through Marielle's and led her to the sofa in front of the fireplace.

"Sorry," Keke said, turning to him. "But this is important. Remember how we changed the setup on the second run today?"

Inigo nodded, but his attention was divided between Keke's explanation of how he could shave possibly up to a second more off his time by shifting at a different moment and watching Marielle pour two glasses of wine for herself and Elena.

Keke kept talking, but all Inigo could hear was the women's laughter. Finally his friend and boss put his arm over Inigo's shoulder. "You okay?"

"Yeah," he said. He'd just spent the evening trying to convince himself that Marielle was the key to winning and now...he was getting the message that maybe he hadn't thought this through. His gaze drifted over to the women, and Keke noticed.

"It's not always easy to balance racing and a woman," Keke said. "Elena had her own thing, which made it easier for us. Is she the woman that Marco mentioned?"

Inigo turned away from them, walking to his den area, and Keke followed. "I wonder if today was a fluke."

"That's why I'm here. One of the strengths that I had as a driver was the ability to analyze not just the car and the setup but also my physical well-being. What was going on in my head and my body. I stopped by so we could work through that," he said.

"I had spent the night and morning with Marielle," Inigo said. "You know I've been careful about keeping myself focused on driving and not allowing anyone to distract me, but she's different."

"Good. That's the kind of thing you should log," he said, reaching into his jacket pocket and pulling out a small journal. He put it on the desk between them. "This is my journal from the year I won the championship. It's got everything in there. Even the stuff I did wrong. I wasn't on my A-game that year, but I was happier than I'd ever been before, and I think some of that joy translated behind the wheel."

Joy.

Not sex. Inigo flipped open the journal and glanced down at it. Keke was very detailed, outlining everything from the moment he woke up. He detailed his sex with Elena too, which Inigo didn't want to read about. But when he flipped the page, he saw that Keke had then described how he'd felt when he qualified for the race.

"I went back at the end of the race and underlined the things I thought helped me," Keke said. "Marco thinks this is all mumbo jumbo, but racing has never been just about the machine. The driver has as much to do with it. And I think you are on the verge of finally understanding what that means."

"I agree," he said. "Thanks, Keke. I think this will help."

"Good. That's what I was hoping to hear," the other man said, clapping him on the back. "Marielle can make you into a better driver, but watch the balance, because some women can become the kind of distraction that no man wants."

Marielle had more fun with Elena and Keke than she expected to. She'd been exposed to many drivers in her year as a trophy girl, but it had been different than this quiet evening at home. They ended up playing cards with the other couple, and she saw a different side to Inigo. He was relaxed but a little on edge at first, which made sense given that Keke was a former Formula One champ and his boss, but as the evening wore on, he started to loosen up.

Elena had given her some advice about dating a driver. Marielle appreciated it, but it also made her realize that many people didn't know about her affair with Jose. Carlton had done a nice job of covering it up. At the time she'd been ticked off that he'd stepped in, but thinking about how Elena and Keke might have treated her if they knew, she was glad.

And it drove home the fact that if she was going to keep doing this, even just as some sort of friends-with-benefits thing, she needed to make amends with Bianca. She was starting to really care about Inigo, but she had to be careful because she had a way of ruining even the simplest relationships.

"We should be going. I told the sitter we'd be home by eleven," Elena said. "Thank you for helping salvage our night."

"You're very welcome," Marielle said. "I really enjoyed it."

"Me too. You've got my number, so text me. We can have lunch or coffee," Elena said.

"I will," she said when Elena leaned in to kiss her cheek before she and Keke left.

When the door closed behind them, Inigo leaned back against it. "That was unexpected."

"It was. I think they saved our evening," she said.

"I think so too," he said. "Listen, I think I was wrong to suggest we hook up so I can improve my time. I don't want that to be the only reason we are together."

"Me neither," she said. "But honestly, I don't see a way for us to be together. I mean, I'm lucky that they didn't know I had been with Jose, but that is bound to come up at some point. I don't want that to affect how everyone sees you."

He shook his head and then rubbed the back of

his neck. Something she realized he did when he was trying to figure out what to do. They were both caught between the past and this thing between them. It had almost been easier when it had been just sex. But tonight had changed that. She felt like they were becoming friends, and she couldn't hurt a friend.

She had so few, and each of them was cherished. She had to admit this was the first time she'd met a guy who made her feel this way. That didn't mean she was going to pursue it. In fact she was pretty damn sure she was going to walk away.

She had no idea how to handle him. She reflected on their evening with the older couple. What she'd seen between Keke and Elena was different than anything she'd experienced before. She liked it, but they were very domestic and that wasn't where she was in her life. She'd pretty much decided that marriage wasn't for her. And could she be satisfied with anything less? Would he?

He'd just asked her to hook up, so she guessed he'd be happy with much less.

"It's too bad that we can't just…never mind," he said.

"What? Don't turn shy on me, speedy. You've never hesitated to say what's on your mind."

He shrugged. "I was going to say sneak around, but I don't think either of us would enjoy that."

"No," she said, turning away from him and walking back to where she'd left her bag. She didn't want to be his secret lover. She'd done that before. "I think this really is goodbye."

She turned to face him and then walked over to grab her coat and the container of leftovers the chef had prepared for her before he'd gone home for the evening. She put on her coat as Inigo stood near the door watching her as if he wasn't sure what to do.

But she was taking herself out of this equation. She'd had enough of this world. That confidence that had come from her early-morning discussion with Inigo was all she needed to make herself move on. This was fun right now, but history had taught her that it would become toxic in no time at all.

"I hope you continue to post those faster times," she said. "I think this year is going to be a good one for you."

She leaned over to kiss his cheek, but he turned his head and their lips brushed against each other. She deepened the kiss without thinking, thrusting her tongue into his mouth as she angled her head to grant her more access. She put her free hand on the back of his neck and enjoyed every second of the kiss before she stepped back.

"Good night."

She opened the door and walked away without looking back. She knew she'd made the smartest decision in her history of dating. Though she had a few twinges of regret thinking she could have hooked up one more time with him, she knew in the end this move had been the best one for her.

Her sleep that night was restless, and she dreamed of Inigo's touch on her body, waking in a fever for him, but that was something she was going to have to live with.

Twelve

"Thanks for adjusting your schedule to mine," her mom said as Marielle showed up for tea at the Waldorf the next afternoon. Their plan to meet at Ralph's yesterday had fallen through when her mother's lunch ran long. But she never missed a chance to stop by the Waldorf when she was in town, so this was the perfect chance to catch up.

"Not a problem," Marielle said, sliding into the chair across from her mother. "I'm sorry that things got so out of control the other day on our call. I know that your events have a certain standard to them, and I realized that I don't want you to compromise anything to include me."

Her mother leaned back in the chair, her eyes narrowing a bit. "I'm not sure if you are serious or not."

"I am," Marielle said. "The thing is, if you included me with the other influencers, it would be a nice bump in my profile, and I think it might bring me some more luxury brands as sponsors. But at the same time, it wouldn't hurt me to build my following and work to increase my numbers on my own."

Her mom nodded. "Your social media handle was on the list of influencers that the charity thought should be invited, so someone thinks you are ready to move to the next level."

"I'm glad to hear that. I know you haven't had a chance to see what I do on social media," she said. "Maybe you'd like to accompany me to an event, so you can observe me interacting and see how I translate the event to my followers."

Her mom seemed surprised for a split second before she hid it. "I'm not sure that my schedule will accommodate that. I've had a look at your social media sites and really like what you are doing with those stories. I was surprised at how real it felt when I watched it. I liked what you did with your posts about New Year's Eve."

"Thank you," she said. "Most of that was Scarlet's idea. She's been mentoring me as I'm working to learn the right way to build my followers. She said to be authentic but also make sure to put limits in place. She's kind of a trailblazer when it comes to this. She started out with her reality TV audience and has been growing it since then."

Marielle didn't mention that she hadn't had a chance to talk to Scarlet since New Year's Day, when the thing with Bianca had happened. She wasn't about to tell her mother about that. Her mother had liked Jose when Marielle had brought him home that one time, but when he had died, and her parents had realized that Jose was married, they'd been horrified. Especially her mom, who had been cheated on by Marielle's father.

Her therapist had asked if she'd had the affair to make a statement to her mother. Had it been a passive-aggressive move? But Marielle couldn't make that connection. Other than wanting to be as different from her mother as she could be. She knew she couldn't bring that subject up at their meeting. Maybe later she'd talk to her mom about the fallout on New Year's.

"That's really nice of her. She's on my list as well. Perhaps you two could come together. Many people know that you're friends, and I think that would be a nice workaround for the situation. You and I can be ourselves without having to make a public statement about being mother and daughter. Would that work for you?" she asked.

It was more than she'd hoped for, and Marielle nodded. "Thank you."

"No problem. I was impressed that you didn't go to Dare to solve this for you. I thought about that a lot after your call. I know that there are times when our relationship has been strained, but coming to me on your own really meant a lot to me."

"Me too," Marielle said. "I recently met someone who made me look at myself in a new way, and it really has helped me a lot."

"I'm glad to hear that. Who is it?"

She wasn't prepared to talk about Inigo and had surprised herself that she'd even mentioned him. "Just a man who was at Scarlet's party. He was funny and charming, and he saw me not as Marielle Bisset but just as a woman. Does that make any sense?"

Her mother laughed and nodded. "More than you can know. It's nice to just be a woman every once in a while. Reminds us of who we are when we aren't in the spotlight that follows your father around."

"Exactly," she said. They finished having tea, and her mother gave her a hug before she left. Marielle was about to get in a cab when she felt someone watching her. She glanced up to see that it was Elena, Keke's wife. She smiled and waved.

"How do you know Juliette Bisset? I've been trying to get a meeting with her to see if she'll use my swimsuit line at her summer Hamptons party, and she always says no."

"She's my mom," Marielle said.

"She is? You seem so…different. God. Listen to me. I think I've spent too many hours with this one," Elena said, lifting a cute little toddler into her arms.

The boy had white-blond hair and Elena's striking eyes. He smiled at Marielle, and she smiled back.

"It's okay. My family is complicated, and so is my mother. I've spent my entire life trying to not be like her, so it is a compliment of sorts."

"I'm glad to hear that. When I first started modeling, I didn't speak English, so everyone thought I was a frosty bitch. It took a long time to shake that image. I guess what I'm saying is that I completely get what it's like to have people think you are one thing and knowing it's not you."

"Thanks, Elena."

"You're welcome," she said. Marielle had that feeling again like she had turned a corner, and she liked it. She'd had a meeting with her mom and hadn't ended up saying something she'd regret later. No matter what else happened, she owed Inigo for that.

Inigo's times weren't as good as they had been the day before, and he wanted to blame it on the evening he hadn't spent with Marielle. But he knew it was just because he wasn't connected to driving today.

And now he had another problem. Bianca had seen the picture of him and Marielle kissing as they got into the car the other night. She'd texted him first thing, but he hadn't responded.

Marielle had been right when she'd said there was no way they could have anything together. He knew that. But he also wondered if there were some way that Bianca could meet her…and then what? His sister was never going to see Marielle as anything but Jose's mistress. She'd never know that crazy sense of humor she had that always made him laugh.

Nor should she have to. Bianca had struggled to find her happiness, and she was truly in a good place with her marriage to Derek. Her son, Benito, had happy memories of his daddy because Bianca hadn't wanted to take that from him, and she was expecting another child.

They were doing well. And Inigo, who'd spent so much time going after what he wanted and not really considering how it affected his family, wasn't going to be the one to rock the boat.

"What is going on today?" Marco asked, coming over to the simulator. "Take a break and get your head on right. If you drive like this, we'd be better to send Keke's three-year-old to the race."

He nodded. "Sorry. I'll do better next time."

Inigo walked out of the simulator room and hurried into the small room that had been set aside for him. There was a couch where he'd tossed his duffel bag when he'd arrived this morning. He took out his phone, accessing his playlist, and as he did so the empty notebook that Keke had left for him fell out. He picked it up, grabbed a pen and started writing down everything.

The mixed feelings he had about letting Marielle go. How what he'd learned about Jose was making him question so many things that he'd always taken for granted. How he could have known the man as well as he thought and never realized he was cheating on Bianca.

And he had never suspected it. He hadn't seen Marielle or any other woman, but it had been clear when Jose had died that there had been many women.

He thought about what Keke had said. Joy had been what helped him drive better, but joy didn't seem like something that Inigo could easily access. Instead he thought of the day before and that chill feeling that had swept through him when he achieved his best times. He knew that it had been the sexual satisfaction that had started it. He closed his eyes, leaning back against the wall as the playlist switched to the songs that had been playing in the club when he'd danced with Marielle. Pitbull, as always, sang the soundtrack to his life, and now Inigo pictured Marielle in his arms on the dance floor.

He remembered the faint smell of alcohol and sweat and her fresh flowery perfume. How she'd felt as her body had brushed against his.

He took several deep breaths and pushed out all the baggage that came with being with her and stood up. He just wanted to remember how he'd felt in that one moment with her in his arms.

He remembered how she looked as he'd made love to her. His body shuddered with the memory of how perfectly she fit him.

He walked back into the simulator room and nodded to Dante, who was lounging against his workstation. Dante called for everyone to get into position as Inigo walked to the simulator and got in.

Immediately he felt a difference in his performance. He had no idea if his time would be as good as the day before, but he realized that he was figuring out something about himself. The driving couldn't be separate from his life. He couldn't isolate himself from the world in order to drive faster. Until now, he'd cut himself off from women, drinking, family time. While he wasn't going to start drinking again, maybe it was time for him to start living. To find a way to blend the two.

The way that Marielle had done for him. He knew it hadn't been her intent, but she'd forced him to see the link between racing and his family. When he stopped and got out of the simulator, he glanced over at Marco.

His boss nodded and gave him a thumbs-up sign. "Better. Keep doing that. Whatever it is that you did at the end. That is the key for you. My brother needs me back in Milan, so Keke will stay and send reports to me. I like the way you are improving, Inigo. For each driver, the key to winning is something different. It's not something that I can tell you or even Keke, for all his wisdom, but to me it seems as if you are getting closer to that."

He nodded. "I am. I'd like to take a few days off over the weekend to go home. My sister is close to delivering her baby, and I'd like to be there for that."

Marco took a deep breath and shook his head. "Will it interfere with your driving?"

"Honestly, I think it might help it. I need to keep living. I've been too isolated, and it isn't really helping me to win."

"Okay. You're from Texas, right?"

"Yes. Why?"

"I'd like to see you out on a track getting some real-world practice. I'll have my assistant see if you can get some time at the track in Austin. Sound good?"

"Sounds perfect," he said.

Marco left, and Inigo realized for the first time since he'd started racing, he felt comfortable being a driver. He'd always thought the approach he'd been taking would bring him the results he wanted, but it hadn't.

Not until now. Not until Marielle.

Two days later Marielle was at a party at Siobahn's to celebrate the release of her latest single. Marielle had done a live video and her followers loved it, then she'd taken a break and was sitting in a quiet corner trying not to do a search on Inigo. She missed him. Yet at the same time, she was trying to remind herself that she didn't need him.

"Hey. Do you mind if join you?" Scarlet said.

She was in her second trimester and had a cute baby bump but still managed to look like the hellion she'd always been.

"Sure. How are you doing?" she asked as Scarlet sat down next to her.

"I'm good," she said, rubbing her stomach. "I wanted to see how you were. I know that things didn't end so well on New Year's Day. I haven't had time to call…well, that's not true. I wasn't sure what I was going to do at first. Alec and his family see you as some sort of femme fatale and think you should have a big scarlet letter on your chest."

Hearing what she already knew said out loud was like a little wound to her chest. It hurt, but it also made her angry. "Whatever. It's not like I want to be in their lives."

"Well, not all of their lives," Scarlet said.

She nibbled on her lower lip, turning her head to the side. Yeah, not all their lives. Just Inigo's. "That's over."

"Is it? I saw a photo of you two not that long ago on TMZ. And honestly it was that picture that made me realize that Alec was being stupid. I mean, you two were really into each other. And why shouldn't you have a chance at that? Why should I be mad at you for something that happened before either of us knew the Velasquez family?"

Marielle couldn't help smiling at the way Scarlet said it. She put her arm around the other woman, hugging her. "Thank you. That has to be one of the nicest things anyone has ever said to me. It means more than you know to hear that. I don't think Inigo and I will ever be together, but still it's nice to know you had my back."

"No problem. As troublemakers, we have to stick together," she said. "Plus, Siobahn read me the riot act. Her point was, since when did I let past mistakes define how I look at a friend. I know you regret falling for Jose's lies, and if Bianca ever met you she'd realize that you beat yourself up for that still."

Marielle had to laugh. Siobahn was still down on guys after her ex had married someone else mere weeks after dumping her. "She sees the world from a unique vantage point right now."

"That doesn't mean she's wrong," Scarlet said.

"Don't let her hear you say that. It will go to her head."

"Whose head?" Siobahn asked, coming over and sitting down next to them.

"Yours."

"My new single rocks, doesn't it?"

"It's a revenge song... I think when Mate hears it, he's going to lose his shit," Scarlet said. "Wish there was a way to see his reaction."

"Oh, there will be. He's doing red carpet for that movie he wrote the soundtrack for. I'm sure it will come up," Siobahn said.

"How can you know that?"

"I was on a morning radio show this morning and hinted it was about him without saying it," she said. "Life is good."

Marielle knew that feeling. It was hard having

your heart broken and feeling so low. Though she wasn't the kind of person who wanted some kind of public humiliation for her exes, she understood why Siobahn did.

"How's things with the race-car driver?" Siobahn asked. "You could have brought him."

"We're not together," Marielle said. "It was a hot mess when we tried to figure out how it would work, and we both walked away. It's better."

"I saw you two—"

"Don't, Siobahn. I know you mean well, but there's no way that we can be together. My life is finally not the cray-cray show it always has been," Marielle said.

"Fair enough. I just know you. You looked like you were starting to fall for him."

"Probably all the more reason for us not to be together," Marielle said. "When has love ever ended for any of us in anything but disaster?"

"Uh, excuse me. I'm rocking happily-ever-after," Scarlet said.

"You are. You're the exception that proves the rule. Siobahn and I can't chance it. We might jinx you," Marielle said.

"You won't jinx me. But I do like the idea of you getting you right before you add a man to the mix. For me I had the pregnancy, so I had no choice but to figure out how I could make it work with Alec. And you know, I'm glad I didn't have too much time to think about it. That man might make me crazy sometimes, but I've never felt so happy and in love in my entire life. And he actually loves me."

"Of course he does. He'd be an idiot not to," Siobahn said.

Marielle hung out with her friends for the rest of the evening, and when she went home, she told herself that the empty apartment didn't bother her. She was strong and independent. She didn't need a man. In fact, she'd never really needed anyone else. But that didn't mean that she didn't miss Inigo.

He had a way of making her laugh at nothing. She stood at the window and remembered standing by his, seeing Central Park from the other side. Tonight, there wasn't as much snow, but she wasn't looking at the park. Instead she tried to see all the way to the other side and the man she was trying to convince herself she didn't miss.

Thirteen

Breakfast at Peacock Alley in the Waldorf Astoria was both elegant and refined. Inigo had never been before, but Marielle knew the maître d' and had gotten them a table that was out of the main dining room and quiet. She looked different than what he'd come to expect today. She was still herself, but she'd braided her long blond hair and a few tendrils had escaped to frame her heart-shaped face. She smiled easily, but he could still see some signs of tension in her expression.

He felt it too. Accidentally running into her at Ralph's when they'd first reconnected had been one thing, but this…he was now back to toying with an idea he wasn't sure he could commit to.

Revenge had been an idea that he'd toyed with but his heart wasn't in it. As much as he thought Marielle needed to be brought to see how badly she'd hurt his sister, he couldn't stay away from her. He was in the crosshairs of a dilemma like he'd never experienced before. He'd always prided himself on being a man who put family first, but here he was with Mari. Again.

He'd finally answered Bianca's texts. To say his sister was upset about the TMZ photo of him kissing Marielle was an understatement. She had gone into brutal detail about what had happened with Jose. Now Inigo was torn. Part of him was still so angry about how Bianca had been treated by Jose and his mistress. But another part of him looked at Marielle and had a hard time making the connection between any viciousness on her part and the hurt and guilt that were in her eyes so often when she spoke of Jose.

He needed answers, which was why he'd asked Marielle to meet him even though they'd agreed not to see each other anymore. He had to ascertain if she was the heartless other woman or Jose's victim. He'd seen Jose use his charm to soothe angry race officials and tempt fans over to their team. He'd been larger than life and Inigo had been in awe of the man. He had wanted to be like him when he grew up. But now...

Feet of clay, he thought.

"I'm not sure I've ever been with a guy and not

talked for this long," Marielle said. "You're very serious this morning."

"Got a lot on my mind," he said. "And I was checking out this place. Not many restaurants like this in Cole's Hill."

"My family has been coming here for Sunday brunch for years. We have a history with this place. After we eat, I'll show you the portrait of my paternal grandparents with the former owners that hangs in the owner's lounge."

"I'd like that. Is family important to you?" he asked, as one of the waiters poured him some coffee.

"I'd like to say no, but that's not true. As much as I try to do things to shock my parents, I do love them," she said.

"Was the affair with Jose something to shock them?" he asked.

She tipped her head to the side. "Are we going to talk about that again?"

"I think we have to," he said. He'd always been direct, and he couldn't imagine that he was going to change now. He wanted to understand her. To try to reconcile the lover who'd been in his bed on New Year's Eve and the woman he'd learned she was the morning after.

"Of course I wasn't doing it to shock my parents. It was because I thought I loved Jose," Marielle said with a shrug. "I never would have gone into that relationship if I hadn't believed him when he said his marriage was over."

"Do you regret the affair? Now that you know about Bianca?" he asked.

She picked up her mimosa and took a sip. "How can you be asking me this? I already told you how much shame I feel."

"Bianca saw a picture of us kissing when we left the Polar club the other night, and she isn't happy. She's been telling me more about what happened," he asked.

"Is that so? Well, you should just remember that there are two sides to every story," Marielle said. "Not that I blame her at all. But he lied to both of us."

Inigo felt the slow burn of anger. The fact that Marielle seemed to have no shame about her actions made him realize that his attraction was a mirage. He might be seeing something in her that wasn't real.

Sex. He had to remember it had been a year since he'd gotten laid before Marielle. Maybe that was responsible for his obsession with her.

"I'd think you'd have some regret. She was pregnant."

"I can't control anyone other than myself. I was upset and broke things off when I realized that Jose was lying to me," she said. She chewed her lower lip and looked away from him. "He made me promises as well. But he wasn't a man of his word."

That didn't jive with the Jose he knew, but Inigo had realized after his mentor's death that there was a lot about him that he'd never known. He'd only seen

Jose's talent as a driver and knew that if he wanted to be the best, he needed to emulate what he saw.

On the other hand, he didn't feel as if he knew Marielle at all. She seemed so callous toward Bianca and took no responsibility for the outcome of her affair. That affair had devastated his sister. Inigo wondered if someone treated Marielle that way, she'd finally be able to find some empathy for Bianca.

And worst of all, Inigo still wanted her. Could he have her? Or was avenging his sister the right course after all? He'd been so worked up after his call with Bianca that he hadn't even thought about how all this might impact his racing.

"Did you only ask me to lunch to discuss the past? Because if so, we're done here," Marielle said, shifting in her chair as if she were going to get up and leave.

"No, I want to discuss the future," Inigo said, stopping her. "I need you back."

Marielle showed up twenty minutes early to her dinner date with Inigo, which wasn't like her. She almost had her driver circle the block a few times so she wouldn't be early and realized she was nervous.

What did it matter?

He was just a guy.

She hadn't been able to resist when he'd asked to spend more time with her. She scolded herself for giving in to temptation and knew that the situation with Bianca meant that it wouldn't last. But she couldn't lie to herself. She'd missed Inigo. She had to see where this went, even if it didn't end well.

She glanced at her phone and decided she could play this off if she used it for her social media channel. Her manager had noted that her live videos were the things that really got the most views.

She took a deep breath and then asked the driver to stop. Living her best life on social media was always easier than her reality.

The restaurant Inigo had chosen was very popular, and there was a line outside. There had been a light snow falling, and it was almost too perfect. It was the kind of wintry evening that was made for romance. There were some carriages lined up to take couples through Central Park, and she used them as the background, adjusting her position to find the best light for her video.

Then she took a deep breath and turned on the live video feed. She waited a moment for the feed to start and then smiled at the camera.

"Hello, everyone. This is the perfect night for romance and wintry fun. I am in Central Park waiting for my date, and this light snow has started to fall. For a long time, I saw snow as something to be avoided. I always used to worry that it would ruin my hair, make it frizzy, or that the snow would leave wet stains on my clothing."

She tipped her head back and let the snowflakes fall on her face. She'd been so shallow.

"Now when I think of all the moments like this

that I never let myself enjoy, I regret it. I was so obsessed with getting the perfect picture to share, with making sure that everyone thought I had a better life than I did, but the truth is, I wasn't living it. I was staging it, and in the end I wasn't a very happy or nice woman. I hope that if you are watching this, you will get out tonight. Go and enjoy the evening wherever you are and don't worry if it's not perfect. If your hair is a little frizzy or your boots get muddy, that doesn't matter. Are you with the person you love? Someone who makes you laugh? Or even just on your own, enjoying what the evening can provide?"

She noticed that people were watching her, and she just smiled as she twirled in the snow. "Don't let anyone steal your joy tonight."

She turned off the camera and walked back toward the restaurant. That's when she saw Inigo standing a few feet away wearing a black wool coat. He was watching her. She knew she didn't look as good as she had earlier; she could feel the cold on her face and imagined her cheeks and nose were probably red. But the snow and the magical atmosphere this evening had taken away her nerves.

Just letting go of perfection was bringing her a satisfaction she hadn't been able to find before this.

"Hello, speedy. Looks like I beat you tonight."

He smiled at her and didn't say a word as he walked over to her and took her in his arms to kiss her. The kiss was warm and passionate and every-thing that she wanted but had never had.

She saw the flash of the paparazzi bulbs behind him and wouldn't have minded for herself, but this wasn't something that Bianca needed to see. The fledgling relationship she was trying to build with Inigo didn't need the added attention. But she wished she could just ignore them and revel in the fact that for the first time in her life, she was being deliber-ate in her actions. She wasn't staging her world to seem as if she was living a good life—she was ac-tually enjoying it.

And this man.

This improbable man that she shouldn't be kiss-ing at all. But he was perfect for this night.

She put her hands on his face and deepened the kiss. Then he tipped her back, not breaking the kiss, before lifting his head and looking down into her eyes. "Might as well give them a good pose for their photos."

"Might as well," she said, hoping that she wouldn't regret being so public with Inigo. But it was differ-ent, and in a way this suited her brand, her lifestyle that was a mix of luxury and authenticity.

She took a deep breath and felt something shift deep inside her soul. Some place that had been bar-ren and cold for the majority of her life no longer felt so cold or alone.

He twined their fingers together and led her to-ward the restaurant. She was aware of people watching them, and she realized that for the first time she was the center of attention not because she was outrageous.

"You are such a cute couple," an older lady said to them.

She glanced over at Inigo to see how he took that comment and noticed how satisfied he seemed. Maybe this was more than sex. Maybe.

After dinner Inigo was still not sure how to proceed with Marielle. She was funny, irreverent and sometimes would do things that shocked and turned him on. Like when she ran her foot up his leg to his crotch as he was giving the waiter his order. And when his voice dropped an octave, she just winked at him.

But at the same time, there was Bianca and what Marielle had done with Jose. Was Marielle the shallow, callous woman she'd seemed to be in that situation? Should Inigo be the brother who was there for Bianca this time instead of the one who was...well, oblivious to what was going on?

But Marielle had him in a sensual daze. He'd found his own hand up high on her thigh as they'd shared a decadent dessert. And when he paid the bill and led her outside to the waiting car and paparazzi, he didn't think about Bianca or revenge. In a fevered state, he'd pulled Marielle into his arms, his hand sliding under her coat to hold her to him as he kissed her the way he'd wanted to since the very beginning of the meal.

The flashbulbs of the paparazzi who had been following them around brought him out of his sensual haze. He lifted his head and looked down into Marielle's upturned face. He went back to how he'd felt before talking to Bianca this week. He couldn't follow through on his callous plan. He couldn't hurt Marielle the way he'd intended. His tit-for-tat idea of hurting her after making her fall for him wasn't going to bring him any solace or give his sister the peace she needed.

His family were going to see these photos, but he would have to deal with the consequences. Before he might have used them as part of a plan to publicly dump and embarrass Marielle, but now he had no intention to.

"What's going on, speedy?" she asked once they were in the car.

Her nickname for him almost made him smile. "I can't keep doing this. I think you and my sister need to talk."

She shifted completely off his lap and turned to stare out the window. The lights of the city illuminated her reflection, and what he saw made him realize how difficult this was going to be.

"Why? What purpose will that serve?" she asked.

"I like you, Marielle," he admitted. "And it's not just because of my times behind the wheel. I don't want this to be just hooking up. But it can't be anything more unless you and Bianca…come to some sort of understanding."

"Understanding?" she said, turning to face him. "I didn't go after her husband… Jose hit on me. He told me his marriage was over. I don't think I owe her anything."

"She's never going to see it that way," Inigo said. He was being torn apart by this. How could Marielle not see that?

"I don't care," she said. "I'm not saying I haven't made mistakes in my life, but I'm done apologizing for being alive."

"That's not what I'm asking you to do," he said. This wasn't going the way he'd hoped. "Forget I mentioned it."

"How can I forget it? It's always there between us. As you said, there is no way to move past this. The one who could have made this right is dead. We both only know what he told us."

She had a point, but Inigo knew there wasn't a way for him to continue in this relationship with her and not hurt his sister. She lowered the divider between the front and back seats. "Could you take me to my place?"

She rattled off her address, and the driver switched lanes to head toward her place. She put the privacy barrier back up. "I think we need a break to figure out what to do next."

He nodded. "I'm going to Texas to do some training at the track in Austin, and then I'll be back here in February for a week before we leave for Melbourne."

"I'm going to concentrate on my career too," she said. "It's finally starting to take off, and as much as I enjoy this, I want to see what I can do with that."

"Fair enough," he said. "I'll get in touch when I'm back in town."

"Okay."

They were silent for the rest of the drive, and when the car pulled up in front of her building, she put her hand on his arm to stop him from coming around to open her door. "Let's just say goodbye now. It's been fun."

Fun?

"Okay."

It was all he could say. He could think of many ways to describe their time together, and fun wasn't one of them. It had been so much more from the moment he'd spotted her at Scarlet's New Year's Eve party. But now it was over. No matter what they'd both said, this was a forever kind of goodbye. And he was just going to let her leave.

Maybe if it was the end of the season or if he had a win under his belt, he would have made a different choice, but he just sank back into the leather seats of the Vallerio sedan and watched her walk away in the slush.

All of the romance of the evening was gone. No more softly falling snow, no more surprise kisses. No more Marielle.

She entered the lobby of her building without a backward glance, and his driver eased back into traffic, taking him toward his home. He let his head fall back and tried to reassure himself that everything was for the best and this was the good life. But it didn't feel like the good life. It felt like he'd made a mistake. But at the same time, what else could he do?

She couldn't see her way to make peace with Bianca, but was that why she'd left? Or was it that she didn't care for him? He might have been pushing for something she simply didn't want.

When he got to his building and went into the lobby, Dante was waiting for him. They had planned to meet at his place to go over the latest results of his sessions at the facility. He was glad to see his friend and head engineer. Work was what he should be focused on.

"Do you have time to talk?"

"About the new setup?" Inigo asked. He needed to talk about racing and get his head off of Mari and those thoughts of what could have been.

"Uh, yeah, of course, what else would I want to talk about?"

Dante seemed a little strange but then started talking about the changes in the cockpit setup and the engine, and Inigo relaxed. Maybe he was being oversensitive after dealing with Mari. After hearing her dismiss what they had as just fun when Inigo was beginning to think he wanted much more.

Fourteen

"Hey, um, Inigo, this is Derek… When you have a moment, could you please call me? There's something I'd like to discuss with you. I'm on call and have surgery this morning, but you can leave a message on my cell or with my assistant. We really need to talk."

Inigo saved the message. Worried something was wrong with Bianca, he dialed Derek's number, but it went to voice mail.

"Hey, Derek. Call me when you get this? I'm leaving my phone on and I'll have one of the engineers get me if I'm in the simulator."

He hung up, rubbing the back of his neck. Worry about his sister was at the front of his mind. He'd been hoping to talk to Bianca about Marielle. Though she still hadn't shown any regret for being Jose's mistress, Inigo was falling for her. He wanted her in his life, but he knew that would never happen if he didn't find a way to make peace between his sister and Marielle.

His timing was bad, though. Bianca was in her last trimester, and if Derek had called, it had to be bad news. He texted his dad to ask if Bianca was okay. He was so nervous, he saw dots dancing in his eyes before his dad's response reached him.

Hiya, son, we had dinner with her last night and she was fine. Do you know something? Should I go over to her place?

His parents would know if something was wrong related to the pregnancy. Maybe Derek was calling about something else. He twirled his phone in his hands, trying to decide how to respond to his dad.

I was just checking in but didn't want to bother Bianca.

How's the training going?

Really well. The new facility is nice. We are going to head to Melbourne at the end of February.

Mom and I want to see you before then.

I will make that happen. I'm coming to Austin for some practice laps. See you then. Love you.

Love you too.

"Inigo, you ready to try this new setup?" Keke asked.

"Yeah. Sorry about that," Inigo said, walking over to Dante's desk, where Keke waited. Both men had a new configuration up on the computer monitor. "Dante, watch my phone. My brother-in-law left me a voice mail on my last run, and it sounded urgent. If he calls again, will you answer it and then pull me out of the simulation?"

"Is it about your sister?" Keke asked, putting his hand on Inigo's shoulder and squeezing.

"I'm not sure. I just don't want to miss another call. She's not in labor and there is no emergency my parents know about, but that doesn't mean anything," Inigo said.

"We've got your back on this. Can you clear your mind?" Keke asked.

He nodded. He wasn't going to allow anything to keep him from another good run. He had noticed that as his relationship—could he even call it that?—with Marielle had developed, he'd been finding a way to clear his head and drive faster. Part of it was focusing on the remembered feel of her in his arms, but a bigger part was just that she cleared his head. Even with the complications of her past with his sister, she gave him something to look forward to that he hadn't had before.

He took his run. Technically he knew he'd done everything right, but he was also pretty sure that his time wasn't that great. When he got out of the simulator and saw the looks on Keke and Dante's faces, he knew his gut had been right. They both just told him to take a break and come back after he'd spoken to his brother-in-law.

Inigo went outside. Late January on Long Island wasn't exactly balmy, but he needed the brisk air to help clear his head. He was worried about Bianca, half in love with Marielle, unsure how to bridge the gap between the two women and what it would do to his driving this season if he didn't get it sorted out.

The easiest thing would be to break it off with Marielle, but he knew he couldn't do that. He no longer just saw the smiley, sexy persona she presented to the world. Instead he saw the woman beneath the surface. The woman who was struggling to get past her mistakes. He could sympathize with her.

Racing had always commanded all of his time and energy, so he hadn't had the misspent youth that his brother Mauricio or Marielle had, but without racing, would he have been any different from them?

His phone finally rang, and he almost dropped it when he went to answer it.

"Derek?"

"Yes, sorry to bother you when you are working, Inigo, but I need to talk to you," Derek said.

"Go for it."

"We saw the new pictures of you and that woman online, and they showed up in the *Houston Chronicle* as well. Bianca is shocked and upset by this, especially since she'd already talked to you about the earlier photos," Derek said.

"She's really pissed, isn't she?"

"Yes, she is, and I don't blame her. I know it's not my place to talk to you about who you're seeing, but is it possible to not do this now?" Derek asked. "Even as I hear myself saying this, I feel stupid. But you know your sister. She's freaking out, and that's not good for the baby or for her. And she's my world…"

He sighed. Maybe there was no choice but to stop kidding himself that he could be with Marielle. He had never wanted to hurt his sister, and there was the complication of being with a woman who made him feel the same burning excitement outside of the track that he did on it. It was hard to handle.

Betraying Marielle would put distance between them. It would definitely put an end to whatever was going on between them, and he wouldn't have to worry about how trying to have a relationship with Marielle would affect his racing season. But hurting her? Could he live with that? Then again, could he live with himself if he brought a woman that his sister couldn't endure into their family? He had started something in ignorance, never guessing that love would hurt like this.

"I know that. I promise you that this relationship

isn't what you think it is. I'm not seeing her anymore. It was…doesn't matter. I'd never hurt Bianca like that and turns out neither would Mari." He couldn't really say that was the reason she'd broken things off with him but he was going to frame it that way.

There was silence on the phone. His heart ached even saying those words, but he knew he needed to do something.

"Inigo, I don't think that's what Bianca would want."

"What does she want?" he asked Derek.

"I'm not sure she knows herself," Derek said. "It would be easier if Jose were still around to talk to. I think what hurts her the most is she never got closure."

"I agree. Jose left behind a mess and we're all still dealing with the wreckage," he said.

"True. Will we see you before you leave for Melbourne?"

"Yes, I'm hoping to come home when Bianca gives birth and mix that with a training session that Moretti is sending me to Austin for," Inigo said.

He hung up a minute later and turned back to see Dante standing there. "So, how's things with your sister and Marielle?"

"Not good. The press keeps running the picture of that kiss even though we haven't seen each other in a while. Bianca is upset by it and I can't do more than walk away. Everything is a damn mess."

"Did you walk away?" Dante asked.

"Reluctantly," Inigo admitted. "Why?"

Dante shrugged. "I might have said something in the bar the other night about Jose and Mari and your sister."

"What do you mean might have?" he asked. This didn't sound good.

"I can't recall the entire night. I remember someone asking me about Mari and I know I said something about the stuff you told me when you were talking about revenge. Dude, I'm sorry. I hope I didn't screw up royally."

"Hell."

"I know."

"Listen, whatever happens, it's on me. I shouldn't have been talking to you about it," Inigo said. He owned his mistakes, unlike Jose who'd just run from them as fast as he could.

"You trusted me," Dante said. "I should have had your back."

He nodded and just turned away. "Want to talk about racing instead of women?"

"Yes. In fact, I think from now I'll stick to cars. I understand them much better than women."

Dante just patted him on the shoulder and led the way back into the building to talk about the setup for the car. Inigo spent the afternoon trying to concentrate on driving in the simulator, but his heart wasn't in it. He thought about the pain in Derek's voice and the hurt he might cause Marielle if he didn't figure it all out. He realized he'd looked at love like a child.

He'd thought he could play around with a complex woman and walk away unscathed, never realizing that he could be hurt by this too.

He finished his laps, and his time was slightly improved, but not enough to make him or Keke happy. Marco was due back tomorrow, and everyone was on edge, wanting to see some major improvement from him.

He got in his car and drove not toward his house in the city but out toward the Hamptons. He needed an escape, but he knew that the road wouldn't take him away from the weight that was heavy on his shoulders.

He turned around at the first exit and headed back toward New York. The traffic was heavy, and by the time he parked his car in the garage under the building, he was irritated with himself and with Marielle. If she'd been willing to meet him part way, this wouldn't have happened.

He walked into the lobby and saw the paparazzi waiting. Some of them were stringers for online gossip websites like TMZ and E! They wanted a story, and were out for blood.

"Is it true that you are involved with Jose Ruiz's mistress?"

Inigo froze, staring at the man who'd asked the question. How had he known? Marielle had never been named in the press. Dante had said he had mentioned it at a bar when he was drunk…who had he been talking to?

"It's Marielle Bisset, right?" the reporter persisted.

"I can't—"

"Can't or won't? Your sister was his wife, right? How did you end up with the same woman? Does she just really dig drivers?"

"Stop with these questions. That's an insult to me and to her. She's not into drivers."

He walked past them toward the elevators.

"But she was Jose's mistress, wasn't she?"

Inigo clenched his jaw to keep from responding and just waited for the elevator doors to open. Once he got inside, he hit the number for his floor. When the doors closed, he punched the paneled wall. He didn't know what kind of story they were going to run. He should call Marielle and his sister and let them both know what was going on.

But at the same time, he didn't want to talk to either of them. He knew that no matter how he sliced it, he was responsible for this. He shouldn't have ever gone on a second date with Marielle. He should never have slept with her and started to care about her. He should have left her alone instead of falling in love with her.

And now he'd never have her. There was no way back from this kind of story.

But how had they found out about Jose? He hadn't told anyone… Was it Dante's slip of the tongue? He was the only one Inigo had told the whole story to. He knew it wasn't Bianca, Derek…or Marielle. It seemed a far stretch that Siobahn or Scarlet would have let the story out. The only other person who knew the details was Dante.

He punched in his lead engineer's number.

"Did you talk to the press?" he asked as soon as Dante answered.

"What are you talking about?" he asked.

"Marielle and Jose. Did you leak that?" he asked point-blank as he entered his apartment and threw his keys against the wall with enough force to leave a mark.

"I must have. I mentioned I was drunk and I know that's not an excuse. I'm so sorry. I never intended for any of this to happen."

"I get that. But I'm going to have to try to fix this…damn, my nephew doesn't know about his father. I know he's only four. But someday he's going to google his name, and this is going to come up. Bianca's going to have to read about it again and be humiliated. And Marielle, who had started to set herself up as a lifestyle influencer, is going to have to start over. How can I fix this?"

"I thought you and Mari were done."

"Hearing these questions and wanting to protect her has shown me that we're not," Inigo admitted, realizing that he'd been running from his feelings since that moment. He should have known there wasn't a fast enough speed to get away from this. He loved Marielle, and he wished there was some way he could fix this for her.

* * *

"Have you seen the news?" Marielle's assistant asked as he walked into her room at 5:00 a.m. He smelled of snow and aftershave, but his hair was standing on end as if he hadn't brushed it. She realized he'd probably doused himself with the scent on the way out of the door. He was usually so well groomed that it was surprising to see him so unkempt.

"What? No. It's an ungodly hour. What are you even doing here, PJ?"

"You need me," he said, sitting on the edge of bed and fumbling around in the covers for the remote control. He pointed it at the TV, which was always tuned to E! "I would have brought you something to drink but, girl, I didn't want to stop on my way over. This is crazy."

Puzzled, Marielle turned her attention to the broadcast. "Breaking news this morning that upcoming social media influencer Living with Mari is actually Marielle Bisset," the entertainment news anchor reported breathlessly.

"That's not too bad. It was bound to come out at some time," she said. "It's not like it was going to take a lot of digging to find that out."

"Keep watching."

"Though her channel is one that promotes both good deeds and clean living, we have learned that she was the mistress of a married Formula One driver Jose Ruiz for the nine months that his wife,

Bianca, was pregnant. Not sure how that meshes with her mission statement but given that she's a Bisset, not entirely surprising. Within social circles she is known for being a wild child and is rumored to be her father's favorite. I think we all remember that her birth followed his infamous affair nearly thirty years ago."

What the hell?

Marielle pulled the covers over her head. A sick feeling was developing in her stomach. This was stuff that shouldn't be coming out now. She rolled to her side, hugging her pillow to her stomach, and wished she was the type of woman who could cry. But she never had been. She couldn't even get too angry, because they hadn't reported anything that was untrue.

But how had they found out?

"Is my phone blowing up?"

"Yes," PJ said. "Want me to handle it today?"

"I don't know. I need to talk to my parents. I don't know how they'll want me to handle it," she admitted.

"Bisset's current beau, Formula One driver Inigo Velasquez, had no comment," the announcer was saying.

"Please turn that off."

PJ did as she asked and then handed over her phone. "It's your mom. Or do you want me to handle it?"

She took the phone from him. "Mom."

"Marielle," her mom said. "How are you?"

She almost cried then. Thank God her mom was always the first to go into crisis mode. "Freaking out. I thought that thing with Jose was buried. I have no idea how it got out. I'm sorry they led with me being a Bisset."

"That was their mistake. Carlton is on his way to your place, and I will be leaving the Hamptons shortly. We are going to come out swinging. Do you have any idea who could have leaked this?"

"No. I mean, there are only a handful of people alive who know about me and Jose," she said.

"The wife. Didn't you say you'd seen her recently?"

"I did," Marielle admitted. Bianca had been mad and hurt, but she had also been pregnant and had a four-year-old son to think about. For the life of her, she couldn't imagine Bianca leaking this to the press.

"Would she do this?" her mom asked.

"I don't think so," Marielle said. "Would you have done it? Years later, would you bring up the woman Dad did his thing with?"

"No. I hate her. I don't even want to hear her name mentioned," her mom said. "I don't want to rule out the wife, but we'll put her at the bottom of the list. What about the driver you were seeing?"

Inigo? "He's her brother. Surely he wouldn't do that."

"Would he have had a reason to?"

"I don't want to believe that he would, Mom. I

mean, we stopped seeing each other to avoid hurting anyone else."

"Okay. But he's still on the list. Who do you know who might be jealous of your success? You have sort of gone big since Christmas," her mom said.

Marielle couldn't think of anyone. But just hearing her mom defending her and helping her to figure this out meant more to her than she could say. Her mom was still talking about influencers who'd tried to get invited to her event when Marielle started crying. It didn't matter who had leaked the negative information. For the first time in her life, she was being treated as a Bisset, not as a mistake or a consequence of her father's misdeeds. And she hadn't expected it to affect her as deeply as it was.

"Thank you, Mom."

"You're very welcome. I know we haven't always seen eye to eye, but for someone to come after you now is not right. I'm a very powerful woman, and when I find out who it was, they will be very sorry they messed with me. Now don't respond to anything until Carlton gets there. He's bringing a PR person who specializes in dealing with this kind of situation. Is your assistant there?"

"Yes, he is."

"Let him answer the door and go out and get whatever you need. Stay put until we get there. We'll take care of this," her mom said.

She hung up a moment later, and Marielle turned

to PJ. "Mama is finally protecting her little cub," he quipped.

"She is. Who do you think would do this?"

She was trying to think of anyone who would want to harm her career, but this felt really mean-spirited—she hoped that it wasn't anyone she knew well. She wasn't too sure that she wanted someone in her life who would do that.

"I have no idea, but we will find out," PJ said.

Fifteen

Inigo didn't really look at his phone screen as he answered the video chat. He'd left a bunch of messages for Marielle wanting to explain and apologize to her, but she wasn't talking to him. In fact, her family PR man had texted him and told him to stop calling.

"What did you do?"

"Nothing. This wasn't me," Inigo said to Bianca, but his sister wasn't having any of it. She'd video called him, and he could tell she was visibly upset.

"There are reporters in Cole's Hill…that hasn't happened since Hunter got married. No one is happy about it and everyone—I mean everyone—is giving me looks like, *that poor girl*. I went from being someone everyone envied to someone they pitied overnight."

"I think you're exaggerating," Inigo said, noticing as the words left his mouth that Derek was moving his hand across his throat as if to tell Inigo to shut up. He realized that he'd said the wrong thing.

"You think I'm overreacting?"

"No," he said in a rush. "That's not what I meant. Listen, Bia, I didn't do this. Someone on my Moretti Motors team leaked it. Back on New Year's Day I thought that I would make things right by trying to get revenge for you. But once I got to know Marielle, I couldn't… That doesn't matter. She won't even take my calls. I've got Alec looking into it. He can find even the smallest trace of information on the internet. I'm sorry for all the trouble this is causing you and Marielle. For what it's worth, I know Jose lied to her too. She didn't know he was still married when she was seeing him."

Bianca's mouth got tight, and then she nodded. "You're right. It is a big mess. But we're going to make sure the person who caused this trouble will never meddle in my business again."

"You bet we are. But are you okay? How's things with the baby?"

"Fine. I'm fine. The baby is as stubborn as Derek and refusing to come out. They are going to induce on Friday," she said.

"I love you, Bianca. I'll be there on Friday if I'm still welcome. I'm truly sorry for all of this."

"Of course you are welcome, you're my baby brother. And it's not your fault, Inigo," she said. "And as much as I wanted to blame Marielle, it's not hers either. We are both still dealing with Jose's crap even though he's been dead for years. Of course, it's embarrassing to have the world know he cheated on me, but I have a good life with a man I love very much, and I'll get over it."

He smiled as Derek hugged his sister and then kissed her. They had what he wanted. What he'd hoped to find with Marielle, he was realizing. He had made a million excuses for why she affected him so much. She was hot; it had been so long since he had sex; she got him because they weren't trying to impress each other. But the truth was he loved her. He'd probably fallen for her the minute she'd caught him staring at her while his dad shoved him toward her.

"How's Marielle handling this?" Bianca asked after a long pause.

"I don't know. She's not talking to me."

"Oh, Inigo," Bianca sighed. "Why? What happened?"

"I couldn't keep on seeing her... It doesn't matter," he said. There was no way that he was telling his sister he'd broken up with Marielle to keep from hurting Bianca.

"Was it me? Did you let her go because I demanded that you stop seeing her? I'm sorry. I know I was freaking out, but now all this mean-spirited gossip has reminded me how much better my life is now. And I bet Marielle's is different too. I remember that she was twenty-one when she was with Jose. I should have been mature about this."

"Thanks, Bia, that means the world to me. But the issue with Marielle is mine to fix. And you were a victim of Jose's lies and Marielle's gullibility."

"Well, fix it," Bianca said. "Do you love her?"

He just shook his head. "I don't know how to fix this."

"If you love her, you should go to her and tell her you're an ass and she was right—"

"Let me handle this," Derek said, taking the phone from Bianca.

"You think you know more than me?"

"No, but I'm a guy, and I know what it's like to have to woo back a stubborn woman," Derek said.

"Stubborn? *Moi?*"

"Yes. Now go," he said, kissing her and pushing her out of the room.

Inigo wasn't sure that Derek had any advice that would help him. He'd screwed up in his own special way. Derek was more mature, maybe even a little old to be dishing out advice to him.

"Dude, I appreciate it, but I got this."

Derek just laughed and shook his head. "You got this? Tell me what you plan to do."

"Figure out how to spin the leak, then take care of it," Inigo said. "Once everything dies down, then I'll text her and try to get back together."

"You're an idiot," Derek said.

"Hey."

"I know I'm not your brother except by marriage, but I meant that in the kindest way possible. You can't let any time pass, Inigo. Go to her. Tell her what's in your heart and make sure she understands you want her by your side."

He looked at Derek. Would that work? "What if she says forget it?"

"Then you take a few days and go back again. Mo knows what I'm talking about. Your older brother did this again and again with Hadley until she was ready to forgive him. I'll tell you something I have learned from your sister. The deeper the hurt, the more you need to make sure she knows how deeply you love her. If you can't do that, if you don't feel as if you can't breathe when you think of the rest of your life without her, then let her go."

Inigo nodded. He did feel like that. As if without her by his side the rest of his life would be the blur that the world was when he was driving three hundred miles per hour. "Thank you."

"No problem. If you need anything I'm here."

"Thanks, Derek. Keep me posted about the baby," he said, ending the call.

He needed a plan.

The beach was deserted in late January as Marielle and her mother walked along the shore. After her mom had fought her way through the lobby of her building filled with paparazzi, she'd decided they needed to be isolated on the family's twelve-acre home in the Hamptons. It had been three days since they had come back here. Marielle was still recovering, and also wallowing in the love and affection her mother was showering her with.

They'd left the house earlier, as Carlton and her father were having a meeting to determine what the best course of action was. In the past she'd have been tucked up in her room feeling scared and guilty, but not today. Marielle realized for the first time what it meant to be a Bisset and have her family behind her. She'd spent the majority of her life trying to shake off her name and her association with them. But letting Carlton take over the entire mess had been a blessing.

Siobahn had driven her out to her parents' house and stayed for two days before she had to get back to New York because she had another single coming out. Her brothers had all rallied around her, and her father was getting the Bisset legal team ready to ruin the life of whoever had leaked the information— something that Marielle really couldn't get behind, because at the end of the day the gossip was true.

Her mom had been the biggest surprise. Ever since they'd come back out to the Hamptons, they'd spent long hours walking together on the beach. Her mother didn't talk much, she just held Marielle's hand and listened. That relationship—that bond— was something she'd never realized she'd missed until now.

On today's walk, her mom let her talk about Jose

and the affair and urged her to try to figure out her feelings for Inigo. Then she just calmly said, "You were a girl who made foolish choices, but now you're a woman. Make wise choices. I had to face my part in your father's affair all those years ago. I'm not saying it was my fault he cheated. That's on him. But… this is the complicated part… I sort of liked it that he was gone and not in my business with the boys. He used to fight a lot with Leo, and I hated that."

"He's still so hard on Leo," Marielle agreed. "Why is that?"

"They are too alike. I don't know what was in Jose's head, and he's not here to explain it to us. My only advice to you is leave it in the past. It's out there, so it can't hurt you any longer. You have a career that will survive this," her mom said.

"Thanks, Mom," she said at last, hugging her mother.

"Now about Inigo…"

"What about him? His sister isn't ever going to forgive me," she said.

"Is that all that is keeping you apart?"

Was it? He had a busy life and schedule. He'd asked her to give him a chance at a relationship, but she'd never been good at them. She really was better in short doses. Inigo's sister made things complicated, but it was the thought of hurting Inigo that kept her from reaching out.

She might have fallen for him, but he saw her as a possible good-luck charm, someone who could help him win. What if she no longer could do that? What if…what if she wasn't enough?

"No," she admitted to her mom. "It's me. I'm not sure I'll ever be enough for him."

"Does he make you feel like you are less?" her mom asked. "I don't know him at all. I did ask around and heard some encouraging things, but that's never the same as knowing a man intimately. Out of the public eye, life is always different."

Marielle linked her arm through her mom's. "He's never made me feel less than. In fact if I'm being completely honest, he sort of makes me feel like it's okay to be the real me. You know what I mean?"

Her mom tipped her head to the side, studying her. "The real you?"

"Yes," Marielle said, realizing how true it was. "You know how I can sometimes do things without thinking them through…well, Inigo just goes with it."

She stopped walking, as it dawned on her that she'd said no to being in a relationship with him not because she was unsure of him but because she was unsure of herself. She couldn't trust that he could really like her. And she knew a lot of that stemmed from not liking the woman she'd been. But since New Year's—since the night they'd first been together—she'd been changing. Some of it had started before all that, when she'd stopped pretending to have a good life and started sharing more honest posts on her social media channel.

Inigo had seen the real her.

And he liked her.

"Good. That's what I like to hear. I'm not supposed to tell you this, but he's called every day since the story broke, and he wants to see you," her mom said.

"Why aren't you supposed to tell me?"

"Carlton said it would be better if we had no contact with Jose's wife's family," her mom said. "Your father agreed, but I wanted to talk to you first. I'm not saying he won't back you—you know your father would give you the moon—just that he wasn't sure if this Inigo was worthy of you. And frankly, neither was I."

Worthy of her?

She couldn't help the tears that burned her eyes and blinked to keep them from falling. For the first time in a really long time, maybe ever, she felt her parents' love. She wasn't that consolation baby anymore. She wasn't the daughter they didn't want but had needed to move away from scandal. And it meant more to her than she'd thought it would.

Her mom hugged her close and then wiped her own eyes. "I'm sorry it's taken us so long to have this conversation."

"Me too," Marielle admitted.

Inigo hadn't liked going to his brothers for advice, but that's how it had worked out in the end. He'd had no choice. He'd flown to Cole's Hill to be there for the birth of his niece, Aurora, and ended up having a family discussion on how he could win back Marielle. Derek's brothers were there as well, so he'd gotten way more advice than he could use. His brother Mauricio and Nate Caruthers had both agreed he needed to get Marielle naked and in bed as soon as he could.

"Remind her how good you two are together—unless you aren't? Is that the problem?" Mauricio had asked.

Which had led to some good-natured fighting.

Derek and his brother Alec had both reminded him to be honest and speak from the heart. Ethan had joked that at least they knew no one was coming back from the dead, which Inigo had to be honest was a complete relief. Ethan's wife's former fiancé had been presumed dead after a plane crash but then it turned out he'd survived. His return had forced Ethan to admit he loved Crisanne and wanted her for himself not just to console her because of what she'd lost.

Finally it had been Diego on the private plane from Cole's Hill back to New York who had offered him the best advice. "Take her back to the beginning. Show her how much you love her and what it means to you that you met her. It's not easy being vulnerable to a woman, but if she knows she's your heart…it makes everything easier."

So here he was in the O'Malley mansion with only their house staff, waiting and hoping that Marielle would accept Scarlet's invitation to an imaginary party. Scarlet had agreed to set Marielle up.

He had asked the staff to direct her to the large ballroom that overlooked the ocean where he'd first seen her. He waited for what felt like hours before he heard the peal of the doorbell, which he hummed along to, realizing it was the O'Malley Beer jingle. Then he stood there tensely waiting. He heard the sound of heels on the marble in the entryway. He hadn't realized he was holding his breath until she stopped in the doorway of the ballroom and he exhaled in a rush.

Her long, silvery-blond hair hung around her shoulders. She'd pushed her sunglasses up on top of her head, which held her hair back from her heart-shaped face. Her lips were full, tempting, reminding him of how long it had been since he kissed her. Her silvery-gray eyes watched him warily, and he reminded himself getting her here had only been step one.

"Seems like someone lied to me about the party," Marielle said. She stayed in the doorway watching him.

"I asked her to do this," Inigo said.

She stood there for a few more moments while he just tried to figure out what to say. How could he make things right? He realized all of the advice that everyone had given him wasn't helping. He didn't want to screw this up but was very afraid he would.

"Why am I here, Inigo?" she asked.

"Firstly, it's my fault that everything came out about you and Jose. I want to apologize for that," he said.

"You leaked it?"

"No. But I had mentioned it to someone on my team and he spilled it—accidentally but still…"

"Not Keke?"

"No, never. Elena really likes you, and so does Keke. He would never hurt anyone," Inigo said.

"Good. I liked them too," Marielle said. "Thanks for clearing that up. You could have left a message with that information."

"I could have. But Carlton told me to stop calling and texting," Inigo said. "And I'm not going to. I didn't invite you here today for that. I just wanted to clear it up before I told you…well, what I want to tell you."

He felt really hot. Like his entire neck and torso were covered in sweat, and she still just stood there watching him.

"I'm listening."

Oh, God. Could he do this? Tell her he loved her? But he knew he had to. He couldn't keep moving through life at Mach 1 and hoping that when he finally slowed down he'd have someone waiting for him.

He had rehearsed some romantic-sounding things but now standing here, drenched in his own sweat, they were gone.

"I love you."

God. He'd blurted it out, just sort of yelled it across the room.

"What?"

"I'm messing this up," he said, tugging at the collar of his shirt and crossing the room to her. He stopped when he was a few feet away, because he caught a whiff of her perfume and it made him remember how her entire body felt in his arms.

"I love you, Marielle. I wanted you to come back here because this is where I started falling for you that very first night when you crooked your finger at me."

"You did?" she asked, arching one eyebrow at him. "Your dad had to shove you toward me."

"Only because I knew that once I went to you, you would be forever in my heart. It took me a long time to realize that, but it's the truth. I love you."

She gave him a sort of sad smile. "But unless I'm wrong Bianca isn't going to be too thrilled to have me in your life and I don't blame her."

"She's—"

"No, we can't ignore her feelings on this, Inigo," she said. "My mom told me she still hates the woman my father had the affair with all those years ago, and Mom never has to see her. How would it be fair to Bianca for me to be in her life?"

"I was afraid you would feel that way," he admitted. "You have such a good heart. Bianca wanted to come with me today, but she's just given birth and travel is out of the question," Inigo said. "But she sent this video message for you."

Marielle blinked at him, then shook her head. "What?"

"Just watch the message and then we can talk," he said, handing her his phone.

She looked at him, hesitating a moment, before pressing the screen to start the video.

"Marielle, I'm sorry I couldn't be there to talk to you in person," Bianca said in the video. "While your affair with Jose was a shock to my system and something that was devastating when it happened, I've moved on to a rich life surrounded by a family that I love. If I know anything about Inigo he wouldn't have continued to see you if there wasn't something special in you. I'm not saying you and I are going to be besties starting tomorrow but I would like to get to know you better. I forgive you."

The message ended and Marielle let her hand holding the phone fall to her side. There were tears in her eyes as she looked back over at him.

"Thank you for this," she said.

"You're welcome. I love you, Marielle, and there is nothing I won't do to get you into my life. That is, if you want me."

She crooked her finger at him.

He closed the distance between them, stopping when they were only a few inches apart. He was waiting but his heart was full of hope.

"I love you too, Speedy," Marielle said.

He lifted her into his arms and kissed her. It didn't matter when they both knew it, just that they had admitted their feelings for each other.

"I know it won't be easy, but I want… I want us to spend the rest of our lives together. We can figure it out as we go along," he said.

"I like that idea," she said.

Epilogue

One year later

The past year of Inigo's life had gone by at a fast pace. He'd won several races during the Formula One season and had finished in the top five. Keke and Marco were both overjoyed with that result and were looking at ways to improve for the coming season, but everyone agreed he was on the right track. Everyone had said that his happiness off the track had brought him the results he'd never been able to achieve by himself.

Dante had left the Moretti Motors team and gone to work in MotoGP. After revealing that he'd been drinking the night of the leak with Curtis Hemlin, another engineer on the team, an investigation had been launched. It turned out, Curtis had been the one leaking Inigo's times to the bookies. Curtis had been fired and was under criminal investigation. Malcolm's undercover gambling had helped them get the proof they needed that Curtis was the saboteur. Dante had offered heartfelt apologies to both Marielle and Bianca, and Inigo was glad the other man had found a fresh start.

Malcolm and Helena had been married in the fall; practically the entire town of Cole's Hill had been there. Malcolm had written his own vows and made Helena and all the women in attendance swoon at his promises to be his own man and try to avoid temptation. Malcolm really seemed to be a new man after all he'd been through.

Most surprising of all, his sister and Marielle were becoming friends. Once the ugliness of Jose's behavior was out in the open, the two women were both able to move past it. Which was more than Inigo could have hoped for.

Now he couldn't help watching Marielle across the room at Scarlet's New Year's Eve party. The last year had been a busy one for her as well. She'd been honest about her affair with Jose, and that had won her more followers because she'd told the truth. She'd taken on more brand work, and Inigo was in awe of how she managed everything.

He noticed her height, as always, but also the way her hair hung down her back. The dress she wore was one of those shimmery shift dresses she favored, leaving the majority of her back bare. Inigo had taken advantage of that all evening, loving the feel of his hand on her bare skin.

The edges of her tattoo were visible. She'd had a tiny race car added underneath the poison apple. She no longer thought of herself as a sinner, she'd told him, now that they were living together in their truth.

Tonight he hoped to ask her to be his wife. The last year had tested them, and they'd found their own way of living together while he traveled around the world and trained and she worked. He was already talking to Keke. In a few years, after he'd won a championship, he hoped to retire from driving and move up into management at Moretti Motors.

"Sweetie," his mom said, coming over to him and handing him a glass of champagne. "I had hoped I wouldn't have to tell you this, but it's time to ask Marielle to marry you."

"Mom."

"I thought you'd do it last year when you were both home for Thanksgiving," she added.

"You can't be in charge of this," he said to her.

"In charge of what, son? You know your mom only has your best interests at heart," his father said as he came over, putting his hand on his shoulder and squeezing.

"I do," his mom said. "You need to put a ring on Marielle's finger. She's not the kind of woman who will wait forever."

"Listen to her, son," his father said.

"I love you both, but I will do this when I'm ready," he said, hugging them. He walked away, a bit irked that they were pressing him on the very night when he intended to propose.

He'd had the ring for three months now, an exquisite bespoke piece that his sister-in-law Pippa had designed for him and had made at House of Hamilton, the royal London jewelers. He'd been waiting for the right moment and knew that it was tonight.

Marielle glanced over at him and waggled her eyebrows, then she crooked her finger at him, beckoning him toward her. He moved slowly across the room, and then when he was a few feet from her, he went down on one knee.

She just stared at him.

"Are you doing this?"

"I am," he said. "Marielle, you own me heart and soul, and I can't imagine my life without you by my side. Would you please do me the honor of marrying me?"

The music had stopped, and everyone had turned to stare at them, but he had eyes only for her. She was the only one here who mattered at this moment, and she knew it.

She nodded. "Yes!"

He got to his feet, took out the ring and put it on her finger. He lifted her into his arms and whispered against her lips, "I love you."

She put her hands on either side of his head and kissed him back long and deep. "I love you too."

Applause broke out, and their families all came over to congratulate them. Inigo's life had always seemed better as he'd raced through it, not letting anything touch him. But he knew that it had been empty without this woman he loved by his side.

* * * * *

*Don't miss a single book in
the One Night series!*
One Night with His Ex
One Night, Two Secrets
One Night to Risk It All

*And coming April 2020,
a new One Night novel...*

*Scandal rocks the Bisset family
at a destination wedding
they'll never forget!*

*by USA TODAY bestselling author
Katherine Garbera.*

*Available
from Harlequin Desire.*

WE HOPE YOU ENJOYED THIS BOOK!

HARLEQUIN® *Desire*

Experience sensual stories of juicy drama and intense chemistry cast in the world of the American elite.

Discover six new books every month, available wherever books are sold!

Harlequin.com

AVAILABLE THIS MONTH FROM
Harlequin® Desire

DUTY OR DESIRE
The Westmoreland Legacy • by Brenda Jackson

Becoming guardian of his young niece is tough for Westmoreland neighbor Pete Higgins. But Myra Hollister, the irresistible new nanny with a dangerous past, pushes him to the brink. Will desire for the nanny distract him from duty to his niece?

TEMPTING THE TEXAN
Texas Cattleman's Club: Inheritance • by Maureen Child

When a family tragedy calls rancher Kellan Blackwood home to Royal, Texas, he's reunited with the woman he left behind, Irina Romanov. Can the secrets that drove them apart in the first place bring them back together?

THE RIVAL
Dynasties: Mesa Falls • by Joanne Rock

Media mogul Devon Salazar is suspicious of the seductive new tour guide at Mesa Falls Ranch. Sure enough, Regina Flores wants to take him down after her father destroyed her family. But attraction to her target might take her down first...

RED CARPET REDEMPTION
The Stewart Heirs • by Yahrah St. John

Dane Stewart is a Hollywood heartthrob with a devilish reputation. When a sperm bank mishap reveals he has a secret child with the beautiful but guarded Iris Turner, their intense chemistry surprises them both. Can this made-for-the-movies romance last?

ONE NIGHT TO RISK IT ALL
One Night • by Katherine Garbera

After a night of passion, Inigo Velasquez learns that socialite Marielle Bisset is the woman who ruined his sister's marriage. A staged seduction to avenge his sister might quell his moral outrage... But will it quench his desire for Marielle?

TWIN SCANDALS
The Pearl House • by Fiona Brand

Seeking payback against the man who dumped her, Sophie Messena switches places with her twin on a business trip with billionaire Ben Sabin. When they are stranded by a storm, their attraction surges. But will past scandals threaten their chance at a future?

In the middle of topping up coffee cups, Jacob hesitated as a chill rippled over his scalp. He shook it off. Found a smile.

"Wynn? That's an unusual name. I'm putting a case together at the moment. The defendant, if it gets that far—" which it would "—his name is Wynn."

"Wow. How about that."

He nodded. Smiled again. "So what does your brother in New York do? We might know each other."

"How many Wynns have you met, again?"

He grinned and conceded. "Only one, and that's on paper."

"So you couldn't know my brother."

Ha. Right.

Still…

"What did you say he does for a living?"

Teagan gave him an odd look, like *drop this*. And he would, as soon as this was squared away, because the back of his neck was prickling now. It could be nothing, but he'd learned the hard way to always pay attention to that.

"Wynn works for my father's company," she said. "Or an arm of it. All the boys do."